# GLOSSARY FOR AUSTRALIAN TERMS

Esky: a portable cooler
Pub: (short for Public House) A hotel, primary function is a drinking establishment and meals.
Bowlo: (short for bowling club) A community sports centre for lawn bowls.
Kitchen bench: kitchen counter.
2iC: A person who is $2^{nd}$ in command/charge.
Ute: (short for utility) Trayback utility
Rouse: (rhymes with house) To scold

# Dedication

To the folks who watch butterflies, and wonder…

# CHAPTER ONE

## *Jack Brighton*

The flight from Melbourne to Launceston was usually uneventful. A quick hour across the Tasman Sea, away from the rat race of city life, back to my home state of Tasmania where the air was clean and the people still said hello.

I'd attended a week-long national meeting for regional managers of the Parks and Wildlife Services. I had the best job in the world, and meetings like that—while good to keep up to date on news and trends—reminded me that my place was in wide open spaces and the great outdoors.

I didn't go much on Melbourne. The nightlife was better for a man such as myself than it was in my hometown, though this trip had been uneventful on that front too. I had to say, being a twenty-eight-year-old gay man in a small country town in the northeast corner of Tasmania, my options were limited. And when I said limited, I meant zero.

I went out every night I was visiting Melbourne, and there were guys interested in one-nighters, but I was done with that. The instant gratification was all good and well, but I would leave with a hollow, detached feeling that never quite went away. I'd hoped to find someone I could connect with, hook up with when we could, talk on the phone, video chat during the week type of thing. But there was not one guy who sparked my interest. I wasn't too happy to have come up empty handed either.

*Empty handed* was the only thing my sex life wasn't.

I snorted at my lame joke, and only then I realised the guy taking his seat across the aisle from me thought I was snorting at him. He gave me a rather dirty look and quickly

1

turned his head and sniffed. I contemplated telling him I wasn't laughing at him, but then he was busy telling the flight attendant to be careful with his carry-on. He was late boarding the plane and he looked flustered enough without me adding to his troubles.

I was soon enjoying the feeling of taking off and heading home, and the guy across from me quickly had his laptop out and was typing away furiously, so I let my head fall back against the headrest and closed my eyes.

After we'd landed in Launceston, I stood up and went to collect my bag from the overhead cabin and accidentally backed into the person behind me. I'm six foot two and kinda broad shouldered, not exactly built for confined spaces.

"Oh, sorry," I quickly apologised, and upon turning around, saw it was the flustered guy from before who thought I'd laughed at him. I offered him a smile. "Not much room for guys my size."

He looked up at me like a rabbit in a spotlight, blinked several times, blushed a deep scarlet from his cheeks right down his neck, and desperately set about shoving his laptop away, all while muttering what sounded like an apology with his head down.

Well, that was an interesting reaction. One that had my attention, that's for sure.

I took a moment to look him over. He was maybe five ten, thin build, with short brown hair parted on the side and combed to perfection. He had pale skin, the pinkest lips I'd ever seen on a guy, without lip gloss anyway. Which I wasn't exactly opposed to, just so you know. But this guy was wearing a chambray business-style shirt with a navy bow tie.

A goddamn bow tie.

If I were to look up Hottest Fucking Nerd On The Planet, this guy's photo would be it.

Like seriously. He made my insides do stupid things.

He looked back up at me, and I couldn't even be embarrassed that he'd caught me ogling. He didn't seem too happy about it, frowning as he slid his blue blazer on. He put his head back down, trying to make himself smaller, tucked his laptop bag under his arm, and bustled past the people trying to disembark.

And I stood there with my mouth hanging open like a Neanderthal.

With a shake of my head, I got my gear together and waited my turn to deplane.

Man, why couldn't I have met a guy like that in Melbourne?

Putting it down to shitty luck, I got off the plane and collected my suitcase from the Arrivals carousel. But as I was walking toward the exit, I saw bow tie guy at the car rental kiosk and he seemed to be flustered. Again. Maybe flustered was how he got through his day, but he really didn't seem to be having a good one at all.

"I'm sorry, Mr Gale," I heard the car rental lady say. "There seems to be some mistake. We don't have a booking and all vehicles are taken."

Bow tie guy, whose name appeared to be Mr Gale, had both elbows on the counter and let his head fall forward. With a deep breath, he looked up. "Well, what am I supposed to do? I have an appointment at the museum in forty minutes. I need the vehicle because I can't very well take my suitcase to an appointment with a professor, can I? And I'm supposed to be staying out of town, which I obviously will need to drive to. Surely there has to be another vehicle?"

She made a face. "Sorry. But we don't have a booking. Can I suggest a taxi?"

I almost laughed, because good luck getting a cab from the airport to a hotel to the museum in forty minutes. The poor guy looked defeated and on the verge of tears.

"It's a very important meeting," he said weakly.

Before I knew what I was doing, I stopped beside him. "Sorry for intruding. I couldn't help but overhear. I'm headed your way if you need a lift?"

# CHAPTER TWO

### *Lawson Gale*

"I beg your pardon?" To say I was surprised by the interruption was an understatement. Not so much the offer, but who it was from.

It was the man from the plane. The one who'd laughed at me when I was taking my seat, the same man who'd almost knocked me over when the giant decided to stand in the aisle at the same time as me. It wasn't my fault he was absurdly tall and built like a mountain. And of course he had to be gorgeously handsome with his perfect scruffy brown hair and perfect twinkling brown eyes. And a dimple. Of course he had a dimple. It completed his perfect face.

He was wearing a shirt with a Parks and Wildlife emblem over the right breast, dark jeans, and work boots. The outdoor type that worked with his hands was not a look that would normally catch my attention, but it somehow made him even more… perfect. One side of his mouth cranked upwards. "I couldn't help but overhear you, and I'm going your way if you need a lift."

I stared up at him and his stupidly perfect face.

His brow furrowed. "To the museum?"

"Oh." Right. He'd asked me a question. Or offered me a lift, more to the point. "Well…" I composed myself. "I'm not in the habit of taking rides from strangers."

He found something about this funny because he fought a slow grin and lost. He stuck out his hand. "The name's Jack Brighton. Now I'm not a stranger."

I swallowed hard and looked around nervously. No one seemed to be paying attention. The car rental lady was on the phone to what sounded like another disgruntled customer. Probably the person she gave my car to. I quickly shook the offered hand in front of me. I aimed for a firm grip because I loathed limp-fish handshakes, but I needn't have worried. His hand was warm, hard, calloused… perfect.

"Lawson Gale," I declared. "And thank you for the offer, though it would hardly be wise for me to accept. I've spent a lot of money on education; I'd hate for my epitaph to read that I was indeed an idiot, who rather stupidly got into the car with a man I just met. Who turned out to be a serial killer."

Jack stared at me for a second before he laughed. "Right. Well, I've been assumed to be a lot of things. A serial killer has never been one of them."

I scraped my fingertips through my hair, fixing it into place. A nervous habit I was trying to quell. "I meant no offence."

His smile was warm and wide. "None taken. I'll just be on my way then. Good luck getting to the museum in"— he looked at his watch—"thirty minutes."

I watched him turn and leave, wheeling his suitcase behind him.

*Bother.*

I was out of time. And out of options. I quickly scanned the taxi rank through the large glass doors to find it empty. *Double bother.*

I started after the man I'd just called a serial killer. To his face. His ludicrously perfect face. "Mr Brighton!"

He stopped and turned back to me.

"Mr Brighton, please wait," I said, hurrying to catch up to him while struggling to pull my suitcase and keep my laptop satchel strap over my shoulder. "I apologise for my rudeness, and I would graciously accept a ride. If you're still offering, that is. I'd most appreciate it."

He smiled. "Sure thing. Truck's this way."

I followed him out to the car park where he stopped at a large four-wheel-drive utility with a Tasmanian Parks and

Wildlife logo emblazoned on the side. He unlocked it, then threw his suitcase into the back tray like it weighed nothing.

I looked at my suitcase, which was half my size, and wondered how I could lift it in. Maybe if he put the back tailgate down, I could slide it up...

Without me asking, he effortlessly hoisted my suitcase into the back with his. The muscles in his arms expanded and bulged. He waved at the passenger door. "Well, get in or you'll miss your appointment."

Right, yes. Of course. Clutching my laptop satchel, I climbed in. "Thank you again," I said, clicking my seatbelt in. "I really am very thankful."

"No worries," he said, starting the engine. He shifted the gearstick into reverse, looked over his shoulder closest to me, and backed out of the parking spot. He spun the wheel, slid the gearstick into place, and the four wheel drive lurched forward. It was bumpier than I expected, and louder, but it seemed the outdoor nature of the vehicle suited him.

"You work for Parks and Wildlife," I stated the obvious. I didn't need to be a detective: he wore their shirt and drove their car.

"I do." He smiled brightly as we sped down the highway toward Launceston.

"An interesting occupation," I noted. "Do you favour the flora or fauna?"

"Love it all." Then he chuckled. "You know most people would just say plants or animals."

And there it was. The ever-forthcoming dig at my vocabulary. "I'm not most people."

He just seemed to smile wider. "You certainly aren't."

I feigned interest at the passing scenery instead of trying to pretend I wasn't offended.

"That wasn't an insult," he went on to say. "Just the opposite, actually. I like the way you speak. You're obviously pretty smart."

"Above average IQ, one could say," I offered modestly.

6

Mr Brighton scoffed at me. "Right. And where exactly do you fit on the cognitive designation bell curve?"

I shot him a look. He knew what the measure of IQ was? Normally I would rebuff his question, uncomfortable discussing such matters, particularly with someone I just met. But I found myself wanting to be honest with him. "Genius."

The dimple in his cheek appeared when he smiled out the windscreen. "Thought so."

"Does that bother you?"

"Hell no. Why would it? Believe me, the last thing I am when it comes to a man's intelligence is threatened." He gave me a strange look with a questioning eyebrow as though he was implying something else.

Intelligence was not an issue for me either. I was, however, reminded constantly by those I worked with that I lacked social cues. And heaven knows small talk was not my forte.

"So," he started again. I must have let my side of the conversation lapse too long. "Important meeting at the museum, huh? Is it for a job?"

"Not really. Well, in part, yes." I cleared my throat. "I'm meeting a retired professor from my field. I have a two-week case study as part of my doctoral degree."

"Doctoral degree? As in medicine?"

"Oh no. Not a medical doctor, heavens no. I don't have the stomach for blood." Even the thought of it made me uncomfortable. "I'm a lepidopterist."

He nodded slowly. "And that is…?"

"I study butterflies and moths. Predominantly butterflies."

"Wow. Interesting," he said, seemingly genuine. Most people thought it was cute that I chased butterflies like a child. "They're complex little things, I bet. You know, my favourite animal is a dragonfly. Don't tell my dog that, she'll never forgive me. And I know butterflies and dragonflies are different, but dragonflies are… well, I dunno, they just defy logic."

I stared across the cabin at him. "Dragonflies are an incredible insect. I'm not sure what you mean by defy logic, though. Logic for which purpose? For whose purpose? Because logic is a human reasoning and hardly quantifiable in the *Animalia* kingdom."

He smiled broadly. "I just meant they look like they shouldn't be able to fly, but they can. And they look kinda alien. Not that I've seen any aliens to quantify this generalisation."

I sighed. "I apologise. I don't mean to offend…" I picked at the cuticle on my thumb. "My boss, leading Professor Michael Asterly, keeps reminding me of my inability to hold a conversation. Of course dragonflies can defy logic, and I apologise if I implied it was a foolish thing to say."

Now he laughed. Though it sounded loud in the confined space of the utility cabin, it was a warm sound, and his eyes crinkled at the corners. "I thought we were holding down a conversation just fine. And it sounds like your leading Professor Asterly might not know how to have interesting conversations with intelligent people."

I found myself smiling. "The professor is a smart man."

"But not as smart as you."

I shook my head, unable to draw my eyes away from this confounding mountain of a man who liked dragonflies. "No, he's not."

Mr Brighton stared right back at me and licked his bottom lip. "Um." He cleared his throat. "Well, the museum awaits."

I looked outside, only to find us parked out the front of the Queen Victoria Museum. I hadn't even been aware we'd stopped moving, let alone arrived at my destination. "Oh, right." I grabbed my satchel and quickly checked my watch. It was 11:55 a.m. I had five minutes to get inside. I quickly opened the door, then stopped. "You do know Da Vinci drew the very first design of a helicopter, hundreds of years before the Wright brothers designed the aeroplane, based on a dragonfly?"

The corner of his mouth drew up. "I knew that, yes."

"So maybe the design was not so illogical after all."

"Or maybe Da Vinci thought it was so illogical he just had to see how it worked."

I went to rebut his argument, but the more I thought about his reasoning, the less I could argue. "Possibly."

He grinned like he'd won first prize. Then he said, "You should get going."

Oh, yes. Right. I got out of the vehicle, and before I shut the door, I said, "Thank you, Mr Brighton. I truly do appreciate the lift."

"Anytime," he answered. "And please, call me Jack."

# CHAPTER THREE

## *Jack*

I sat there and watched as Lawson raced into the museum. He appeared to be the picture of perfection, impeccably dressed and not one hair out of place. But I got the feeling he ran late to every appointment he ever made.

He was like no man I'd ever met. Crazy smart—genius, apparently—and absolutely clueless about how gorgeous he was. He dressed like it was the 1920s and he spoke the Queen's English like he'd just swallowed the Oxford Dictionary.

Jesus. He made my chest feel too small for my heart.

I wanted to spend more time with him. I wanted to discuss the illogical reasoning of humans and dragonflies, and why butterflies? I wanted to taste those pink lips and see how far that blush ran down his neck…

By the way he'd checked me out when I bumped into him on the plane and then again standing at the car rental desk, I was pretty sure he was gay. Or interested. Or curious. Or something.

I just had to figure out a way of seeing him again… Then I remembered he'd left his suitcase in the back of my ute. I grinned victoriously, and without knowing how long his appointment at the museum was to go for, I had a reason to sit and wait.

And wait, I did.

Two hours later, he scurried out of the front doors, and he tripped over his feet when he saw me leaning against my ute, waiting for him. He looked around and behind himself to see if I was smiling at someone else, which only made him more endearing.

"You forgot your suitcase," I called out.

"Oh!" He looked horrified. And cute. He hurried toward me. "I made you wait all this time. I do apologise."

"Well, I could lie and tell you it was a terrible inconvenience, but I didn't mind. It gave me a pretty good opportunity to ask you out for dinner."

He stared at me like my words made no sense, then a shade of pink bloomed across his cheeks. "Oh."

"If you want to, that is," I clarified. God, I didn't even know if he was seeing someone… Or even if he was inclined to want to have dinner with a man. "If you're interested."

He stammered, his mouth opened and shut a few times, and his blush deepened.

So I softened the question for him. "I don't get to have dinner with guys who can hold an interesting conversation very often. And that's all it has to be, if you want. Just dinner and conversation. My treat."

He blinked and swallowed thickly. "I… well, I… yes. Yes, I think I'd like that. Though I must warn you, as I said before, my conversation skills are not my strongest quality."

I was grinning. I couldn't help it. "I think we'll manage just fine."

He huffed out a breath, then patted down his already perfect hair, looked around nervously, and smiled.

"Right then," I said. "Which hotel are you staying at? Did I hear you say it was out of town?"

"Oh!" He looked horrified again. "When you said dinner…"

I burst out laughing when I realised what he thought I was implying. "No, no, that's not what I meant. I'll drop you off at your hotel and, like a gentleman, pick you up again for dinner. If that's okay? I mean, I'm not opposed to seeing the inside of your hotel room, but I was actually looking forward to dinner and a conversation too."

Now he blushed a deep burgundy. Damn, and if it didn't disappear down underneath his collar. He looked down the street, anywhere it seemed but at me. "Well, I'm supposed to be staying in a place called Scottsdale—"

"Scottsdale?"

"Yes. Professor Tillman suggested it would be a good deal closer to where I needed to go. But my rental car wasn't available. If we could find another rental place, I'd really appreciate that."

"I can do you one better than that," I said. "I can drive you to Scottsdale."

His gaze shot to mine. "No, I couldn't ask that of you. You've already been terribly inconvenienced."

"I live in Scottsdale, so it's not an inconvenience at all."

He didn't miss a beat. His eyes narrowed. "You told me the museum was on your way when you offered me a lift here. I only accepted the ride because it wasn't out of your way. Now you're saying you live sixty kilometres away? Downtown Launceston is hardly on your way. And what of dinner? You would drive all the way back just for dinner?"

"Yes I would," I said honestly. "It's only a forty-five-minute drive. I make this trip all the time. And the museum kind of is on my way, if I choose to drive through the city, which in this case I did. And who's to say I didn't have something to do here anyway? Maybe my reason wasn't all about you."

This shut him up. "Oh. Well, of course it wasn't."

I tried not to smile but couldn't help it. "But it kinda really was. I only offered the lift to the museum because you were stuck. And because you're very cute, I won't lie. That was also a deciding factor."

He blinked.

I laughed. "You don't get compliments very often, do you?"

I didn't wait for him to answer; I just opened the passenger door of the ute. "Hop in."

I walked around the car and got in behind the wheel while he still stood at the door. He frowned seriously at me. "Are you making excuses about driving to Scottsdale? Is that some ploy also?"

"Nope. No ploy. I really do live there. And my dog is probably wondering where I am. I told her I'd be home today at lunch time." I started the truck. "And what ploy would I have? You've already agreed to have dinner with me."

"I could take that back," he said defiantly as he climbed into his seat. "Rescinding a dinner invitation would be well within my personal boundaries."

I barked out a laugh. "Well, we can discuss your *personal boundaries* over a drink if you don't want to eat." I could tell by the look on his face and the colour he went what he thought I meant by that, which wasn't what I meant at all. It only made me laugh more. "Not *those* kind of personal boundaries. That's not where my mind went, but clearly yours did."

He spluttered. "It did not."

"It totally did. And I'm okay with that. But please, let me buy you dinner first. I'm a gentleman, after all."

He tried to speak but couldn't seem to find the words. So instead, he looked out the window at the passing city. I could see the tips of his ears were pink and he was still clutching his laptop satchel on his lap. I felt bad for taking advantage of his embarrassment, but before I could apologise, he turned to me abruptly. "So we are clear, my personal boundaries are mine to divulge when and where *I* choose fit. Not you. Whilst I do appreciate the taxiing me across Tasmania, which you have graciously afforded me—and I am most grateful—I don't divulge such personal information on a first date. Because I am a gentleman also, after all."

*Nerdy, gorgeous, intelligent, and sassy. God, he just keeps getting better.*

"And you can stop smiling like that," he continued.

13

"No, I'm good, thanks," I said, grinning at him. "You just called dinner a date. I'm well within *my* personal boundaries to smile."

He sniffed indignantly, but now he was trying not to smile. "I think you missed the point."

I was pretty sure I didn't. I was so intrigued by this man, I was excited to know more about him. "So, I take it your meeting with the professor at the museum went well?"

"Very well. He's a very generous man. He's donated a reasonable find of specimen to the museum. He's been a lepidopterist for the better part of sixty years, and his collection is quite remarkable."

"He works there?"

"Not at all. He's into his eighties now. He has simply given his entire collection to the museum and wished for me to see it. For some reason, he seems to have taken a liking to me," he said. "He has asked me to do a field study. Chosen me, I should say. He claims to be too old to be trekking into the field these days, and he trusts me."

"Have you met him before?"

"Not before today. I've studied his works and read his many journals. I attended a lecture of his at Melbourne University."

"How can he trust you if you've only just met today?"

"Because he's studied my work and read my journal entries. My thesis, he said, was brilliant."

He spoke of his own merits without ego. I guess he didn't need to. If he was as brilliant as he claimed to be, it spoke for itself.

"I think he likes the fact I'm not... *cohesive* with my peers," he went on to say. "I tend to speak my mind, which annoys my superiors to no end. I also refuse to blindly agree with their decisions only to further my career."

"What's the field study he trusts you with?"

"Ah…"

"You'd rather not say," I concluded. "He trusts you with it, I get that."

"Thank you." Lawson sighed and studied the passing scenery again for a short while. "It's very dry here. I was expecting Tasmania to be greener."

"The drought has hit hard," I explained. "This is the third year with rainfall well below average for these parts. The west and south coasts haven't experienced any drought at all, but the north and east have struggled. Farmers are doing it tough. Towns have been on level three water restrictions for going on two years now."

"I assume water conservation is a substantial part of your job."

"Yep. You assume correctly. Land, water, ecosystems, flora, fauna. It has to be about conservation."

He smiled at me like something clicked into place inside him. "I wholeheartedly agree."

And driving down the highway at a hundred k's an hour, our gazes locked for just a moment, and something clicked into place inside me.

# CHAPTER FOUR

## *Lawson*

Scottsdale was a small agricultural town. With a population of two and a half thousand people, there was a primary school, a high school, a small supermarket, a pub, post office, a bakery, and not a great deal more. It was very scenic, though. The main street had kept its heritage look with old-fashioned bull-nosed verandas, window shutters, and antiquated signs. It was charming.

"Where am I taking you to?" Jack asked as we drove down the main street.

I took out my phone and read the email confirmation. "Bloom's Bed and Breakfast. It was either that or the pub. I don't fancy the noise of a pub, so I opted for the quieter option."

He smiled knowingly. "The B&B is lovely. Well, I've never stayed there, but it looks real nice and the owners are good people. The pub's not bad, though. No real late nights out here, and never any trouble, if that was what you were worried about."

I ignored his implied question. "Do you know everyone in this town?"

"Pretty much."

"How long have you lived here?"

"Three years. And I love it. It was a helluva lot greener when I moved here. A lot prettier, but I do love it here regardless."

"Where are you from?"

"Hobart. And you?"

"Melbourne."

16

Jack nodded and pulled the ute to a stop out the front of a quaint looking cottage with a Bloom's Bed and Breakfast sign swinging from a post in the front yard. "Well, this is you."

"It is."

"So, about dinner," he started. "I had every intention of taking you somewhere nice in Launceston because I thought that was where you were staying. But now you're staying here. I mean, we can still go back to the city if you'd prefer because our dining options are limited. We have the pub or the corner takeaway shop. Their fish and chips are good, and the bowlo has pretty good Chinese food, but if I were wanting to impress, I'd rather eat somewhere a little fancier."

"Are you?" I asked. "Wanting to impress?"

Jack looked right at me. "Yes."

My stomach twisted in a strange but pleasant way. "Then I shall leave it to you to surprise me."

"Oh good," he said with a laugh. "No pressure then."

I smiled, feeling victorious. Over what, I had no clue. "And so you're aware, my expectations are not directly related to the food we eat, but rather the company. And I'm already impressed."

His smile was immediate and heart stopping. Before I could do something stupid, I unbuckled my seatbelt, pushed on the door handle, and climbed out of the ute. Jack scrambled to do the same, and he met me around my side. He lifted my suitcase out and put it between us, his hands still around the handle. "So, is six o'clock okay? It's three hours away. Is that enough time?"

"Six o'clock would be perfect."

He grinned and stared at me.

"Uh, can I have my suitcase?"

"Oh. Sure." He took his hands off it and wiped his palms on his thighs. "Six o'clock, then. I'll just park right here." He took a step backwards, his smile still in place. He took another step backwards as if he didn't want to turn

17

away from me, and even when he walked around his ute, he still smiled at me. He really was ridiculously endearing. The fact he was as sweet as he was tall was purely a bonus.

I found myself smiling as I dragged my suitcase to the cottage front door. I was greeted by a small, grey-haired woman with rosy cheeks who introduced herself as Nola. After I confirmed my booking and handed over my credit card, she kept eyeing my bow tie. "We don't get many folks during the week. Here on business?"

"Yes." I smiled pleasantly, and she was a friendly woman, but I wasn't one to blurt all my personal details to a stranger. A handsome, mountain-sized stranger with a delightful smile, maybe. But I got the feeling this lady was partial to gossip.

"Did I see Jack Brighton drop you off?"

Yes, gossiper for sure. "Ah, yes."

"Such a nice fellow. Moved here about three years ago. Works in the Rangers offices, lives out on Stanning Road. We didn't give his city-self long to stay before he got bored with it all, but he fit right in from day one. They say it takes twenty years to become a local, but I'd reckon he's as good as one already." She looked around the room conspiringly, like someone might overhear her. "They say he's not inclined to date women, if you know what I mean. Not that that's any of my business…"

It was clear she made everything her business, and it was also clear by the way she was looking at me, she was suggesting he may be interested in men and in particular, me. I'm surprised she didn't wink at me.

"No, not that it's any of your business," I said with a smile that belied my tone. "If you could show me to my room, I'd be most appreciative."

"Oh yes." She didn't miss a beat. She just prattled on about the goings on of Scottsdale as she showed me to my room. "It's a private room. You're the only guest here tonight, and Bill and I are at the other end of the house. You won't hear a peep from us."

"Thank you," I said, opening the door and wheeling my suitcase in. I could see all my personal effects had been delivered, as organised.

"Oh, they arrived yesterday," Nola said, nodding toward the plastic storage tubs. "We stacked them in here for you, but of course we didn't look in them. I didn't want to pry."

That told me she'd looked inside every one. She was still talking, but I needed some time. "Thank you. I do need to rest. It's been a long day."

"Oh, of course. Don't mind me. I've been known to chatter," she said with a grandmotherly smile. "What time would you like dinner served?"

"Oh, I won't be requiring dinner this evening. But thank you."

"Oh."

She waited for me to explain, which I had no intention of doing.

"Well, then. What time would you like breakfast?"

"Seven, if that's suitable."

"Yes, yes. Very suitable." She sighed dreamily. "I must say, it's such a pleasant change to have someone your age who speaks properly. Most kids these days—"

"Thank you, Nola. If you'll excuse me. I need to use the bathroom."

"Oh!" she said and stepped quickly out of my room. "Gracious. And here I am keeping you."

As I closed the door behind her, I could still hear her talking as she walked down the hall. I fell back on the bed, which was surprisingly soft and comfortable. I sighed loudly, taking in the blessed silence. I was lying about needing to use the bathroom, but I wasn't lying when I said it had been quite a day. Not only had I met Professor Tillman and had yet to truly absorb all he'd told me, but I'd also met one Jack Brighton.

And I somehow had a date with him.

19

Me, Lawson Gale. Nerd and brains extraordinaire. The guy who never gets asked out, who never dates. I wasn't a eunuch, by any means, but I wasn't... promiscuous either. I never caught the eye of handsome strangers. Hell, I never caught the eye of any strangers. Yet, despite all odds and reason, he'd seemed quite interested in me.

I wished we'd exchanged phone numbers. I'd call him and advise him not to pick me up for our date. Surely I could walk down to the main street and meet him, away from the prying eyes of Nola Bloom. I'd also be able to ask about what my expected dinner attire should be. I had no idea where he was taking me, if it were back into Launceston for five-star dining or to the park for a picnic.

I really should have asked. And I really shouldn't have been so brazen as to suggest a surprise.

Regardless, by the time six o'clock came around, I was showered and dressed in what I hoped were appropriate clothes. Jack was pulling up just as I walked out. "Perfect timing," he said as I climbed into his ute. The first thing I noticed was his smile. The second thing I noticed was the warm spice of aftershave: subtle but stirring.

"I was hoping to avoid Mrs Bloom," I explained. "I don't assume to know your personal business in this town, but she sure does. She told me she'd heard you don't date women. I'm sorry if you thought your private business was private, but it seems Mrs Bloom has made it... not private."

He stared at me for two long beats of my heart, then he burst out laughing. "Nola Bloom is the town gossip. And I don't hide the fact I'm gay. I never have. As far as I know, the whole town knows I am and Nola would be very upset to find out she'd been the last to hear it officially."

"Oh."

His smile morphed into a frown. "Is that okay with you? That people know? If you're not comfortable with people thinking we're on a date..."

"But we are on a date, aren't we?"

"I'd hoped so, yes."

"Then I don't care. If you're concerned if I'm out, so to speak, then yes. Since I was thirteen. It's never been anything I've had to 'come out' about because everyone who meets me assumes…"

He gave me a tentative smile. "Assumes you're kinda amazing?"

I could feel myself blush. "Ah, no."

Jack settled back in his seat. "Okay, so this surprise date," he said. "I had to pull some strings. But I think you'll like it. At least, I hope you will."

"Am I dressed appropriately?" I'd chosen navy trousers, and a white shirt with a navy and maroon chequered pattern.

He looked at my bow tie, then back to my eyes. "Perfect."

He was wearing tan coloured pants and a black, long-sleeve shirt with the sleeves rolled to his elbows. It matched his dark eyes. "You look nice."

"Thank you." He cleared his throat and started the ute, taking us down the main street. "I had to request a favour or two, like I said. But I didn't want to take you to just any old place." He brought the car to a stop not far from the pub, which I truly hoped he wasn't taking me to.

Jack hopped out of the ute and waited for me to join him on the footpath. He walked in the direction of the pub, where I could hear music and loud voices inside, and my stomach curled. "Are we going to the pub?"

"No," he said. "We're going here."

He was standing in front of the bakery, next door to the post office, which was next door to the pub. There was only one problem… "Uh, Jack. It's closed." The lights were off and the sign across the door very clearly spelled *Closed*.

Jack grinned. "Surprise!"

He pushed on the door, and to my surprise, it opened. He stepped inside and waited for me to follow him. There was a blonde woman behind the counter, whose face split into a massive grin. Jack took a deep breath. "Remmy, this is

21

Lawson. Lawson, this is my dear friend and owner of Scottsdale's finest bakery, Remmy."

"Hello," Remmy said to me. Her whole face smiled, if that were possible. Then she quickly looked at Jack. Something silent very briefly passed between them. "Right. I'll be off. Don't forget to lock the door when you leave." She grabbed her bag and was gone with the jingle of the bell on the door. Jack locked the door behind her, and it was then I noticed the room. There was a small table set for two with a covered basket of baked goods in the centre, some bottles of some kind of drink, and a small white vase with a single flower.

He must have caught me looking at it. "It's a native daisy," Jack said quietly. "The botanical name is *Helichrysum milliganii* or Milligan's everlasting daisy. It's found here in Scottsdale. I thought it would be a nice touch."

I was utterly speechless.

Jack swallowed hard. "I'm not strictly a fancy guy. I could take you to the best restaurants and order the most expensive wines, but you wanted a surprise. And I wanted to do something that shows you who I am. I'm just an ordinary guy, and this is my friend's bakery. Remmy's French, her husband, Nico, is Portuguese. Between them they make the best pies and pastries anywhere. And I thought this would be private."

"This is perfect." I looked at him and had to swallow past the lump in my throat. "And you're not just an ordinary guy."

His smile was pure relief. "You sure this is okay?"

I nodded. "Quite."

He pulled out my seat and I was gifted with a waft of his aftershave as I sat down. "I will admit to being nervous when you pulled up in the street. I thought we might be going to the pub."

Jack took his seat and gave me a soft smile. "Why were you nervous?"

I smoothed out the fabric on my thighs. "I'm not exactly the type of guy welcome at most small town pubs."

"The guys here aren't too bad. Like I said, I've never hidden the fact I'm gay, and no one's ever said a thing to me."

"Because you're over six feet tall and built like a mountain. I, on the other hand, am not. And my fashion sense tends to offend the masculinity of some men." I shrugged. "I also don't find conversation about sport or lewd jokes about women terribly appealing."

Jack fought a smile. "I do like football, though I prefer union, which isn't too popular here. And I'm happy to say I've never heard lewd jokes from the guys here. Not that I frequent the pub too much." He looked at my shirt and tie, then back to my eyes. "I happen to love your fashion sense. I never realised that I would find bow ties so appealing."

I could feel my face heat at his words and was grateful he didn't push it. He simply uncovered the basket between us to reveal a selection of what looked like pies and a folded note on top. "Dinner," Jack said. "I asked Remmy what she'd serve to someone she was trying to impress. She said to leave it to her." He took the folded note and opened it, smiling when he read it. He then handed it to me. It was a handwritten menu.

*Lamb, mint, and honey pastry parcels made with fresh and local ingredients, served with baked vegetable cups. Suggest the local brewed apple cider to accompany. Desserts in the fridge. Enjoy!*

"Wow." It was so personal and so intimate, but relaxed. It couldn't have been more perfect for me. "I didn't know what to expect, but it certainly wasn't this. If you wanted to impress, you've succeeded."

Jack slid some portions of pastries onto my plate. "Remmy deserves the credit. I just had the idea and set up the table, she did the rest." He poured me a glass of apple cider, then himself, and held his glass up. "Cheers."

I clinked my glass to his. "To the most unique first date I've ever had."

Jack grinned. "I'm glad."

I sipped the cider and hummed my appreciation. "This is good."

"It's locally produced, not too far from here, actually."

"You're very proud of where you live, aren't you?"

He nodded. "I love it here. Small towns aren't for everyone, I get that. But I feel a part of the community here. I contribute and am rewarded with friends who make the most unique ever first dates happen." He smiled. "I like the quiet life."

"I can appreciate that. City living has its perks, but it is draining."

"You're from Melbourne?" he asked. I nodded. "So, tell me about you. What's the Lawson Gale story?"

"There's not much to tell," I started.

"You're a lepidopterist with an IQ to rival Einstein. Believe me, there's a lot to tell."

I took a forkful of pastry and meat and savoured the taste before talking again. "Wow, that is exceptionally good." Then I answered his question. "I grew up in Melbourne, lived there all my life. Studied at Melbourne University. My parents weren't too happy about my chosen career but accepted it as my decision." I ate some more, this time of the vegetable cup. It was filled with sweet potato, eggplant, and artichoke, drizzled with feta and balsamic glaze. It was incredible. I got so side tracked eating, I forgot to keep talking.

Though Jack seemed happy to watch me eat. His eyes were trained on my mouth, his lips parted lasciviously. The look of desire on his face sent a bloom of heat through my chest. I wondered if he'd think it unbecoming of me if I stood up, stepped around the table, took his face in my hands, and kissed him.

# CHAPTER FIVE

## *Jack*

I put my fork down and took a mouthful of cider to douse the desire flaming in my belly. If Lawson moaned one more time when he ate or let the fork slide between his lips seductively like that again, I wasn't sure my promise of being a gentleman would be upheld.

Jesus. He was so sexy, and what made him even hotter was that he seriously had no clue how sensual he was.

"I'm sorry," he said, sipping his cider. "This is so good I keep forgetting to continue talking. Please tell Remmy I am duly impressed with her culinary skills."

"I will." I ate another mouthful and swallowed, trying to get my thoughts back on track. "Tell me about your family."

I learned he had a brother and sister, both older than him. He was named after Henry Lawson; his brother, Paterson, and his sister, Mackellar, were also named after famous Australian poets. All three were gifted children. "Needless to say, our time at school wasn't easy. Being the children with unusual names who preferred reading didn't make for cohesive schooling. I'm very close with my brother and sister; we all speak often. Paterson studied nuclear medicine. Mackellar, interventional epidemiological research."

"Wow."

He almost smiled. "My parents had hoped I would study medicine. Anaesthesia and perioperative medicine, to be exact." He made a face. "Though it was not for me."

"Why butterflies?"

Lawson smiled genuinely. "My grandfather started me on it, but I've always been fascinated. As a small boy, I would catch them and watch them for hours before letting them go. They are incredibly complex, yet simple creatures. Brittle to the touch, but can withstand the fury of nature."

He seemed embarrassed by what he'd just said, which saddened me. "Your passion for what you do is a beautiful thing. I'm very intrigued. I'd love to learn more."

He tilted his head. "You would?"

"Yes, of course. Why, is that strange?"

"Well, most men I've dated think it's childish, for one. They don't take my work seriously."

"Well, you've clearly dated the wrong guys. Talking about the study and conservation of an entire species is remarkable."

Lawson looked at me like a fire lit inside him. "Thank you for saying that. For understanding." He swallowed hard and his gaze seemed to intensify. "Tell me about you. Your family, what you do for Parks and Wildlife?"

"I grew up in Hobart. I have two sisters, Poppy and April, a mum and a step-dad, had a very normal childhood. Never liked school much; always preferred to be outside. Somehow got the grades, so I studied Environmental Science at Sydney Uni. Volunteered for the Rural Fire Service, which I still do. I scored an outreach program through Parks and Wildlife, landed a foot in the door, so to speak. Now I have the best job in the world."

"What were you doing in Melbourne?" he asked, finishing his dinner. "For you to be on the plane this morning."

*God, was that just this morning?* "A week-long national meeting for regional managers. They have them every six months or so." I sipped my cider. "I don't mind going, actually. A change of scene is always good, and a taste of nightlife one or two weekends a year might scratch an itch or two but reminds me how much I love quiet nights at home."

He paused for a moment, licked his pink lips, and his eyes never left mine. "So, did you have your itch scratched?"

Fucking hell. When he said his conversation and social skills weren't his strong point, he wasn't joking. He certainly knew how to ask upfront, personal questions without flinching. My stomach somersaulted under his scrutiny. "Uh, no. Not this time. I wasn't interested in anything on offer. But then someone on the plane caught my eye. A handsome guy wearing a bow tie."

"And how's that working out for you?"

I smiled at him. "I'm hopeful that things are going okay."

"I would think they're going better than okay."

I chuckled. "I'm glad I offered him a lift, then."

"I'm glad I accepted. My initial concern that he may have been a serial killer seems to be unfounded."

"I'm glad."

He smiled as he sipped his cider. "Well, someone who knows the local state forests terrain *could* easily hide many bodies."

Now I laughed. "Thanks."

Lawson shifted in his seat. "Tell me about your work. What is it that you do exactly?"

So, over the mini Portuguese tarts I got from the fridge and another bottle of cider, I told him about data collection and collation, water testing, soil testing, animal tagging, writing reports, reading reports, and more data collection. How we implemented action plans and the importance of public information and awareness, and how we correlated the impact humans have on the environment to changes we've seen.

Lawson listened intently, then launched into his own interpretation of ecological system conservation, and how the study of butterflies has shown decreases in habitat and reproduction, how the different species adapted, and how some were disappearing altogether.

I could listen to him speak forever. He spoke with such eloquence and intelligence, it was refreshing. When he was making general conversation, his hands rested in his lap. But when he spoke about butterflies, his face lit up and he used his hands animatedly and lost that inhibition and self-consciousness that seemed to weigh him down.

A knock at the door scared the crap out of us. I checked my watch as I stood up. Jesus. It was almost midnight. *Had we really been talking for that long?*

I peeked through the curtain to find Steve, the local police sergeant. He was maybe fifty years old, fit as a bull, and liked by everyone who met him. I opened the door and offered him a smile. "Steve."

"Oh, hey, Jack. I was passing by and saw the lights on. Thought it was too late for Remmy or Nico to still be here and too early for them to start."

"No, they're not here," I said. "Remmy graciously let me use the shop." I stepped back, allowing Steve to poke his head in.

He saw Lawson sitting at the small table. "Oh. *Oh.*"

I almost laughed at his expression as it dawned on him that we, two guys, were on a date. "Remmy made us some of Nico's Portuguese tarts, and we'll never eat them all," I said, taking the plate with a few remaining sweets. "Please take one."

Steve acted like he wasn't going to take one, but he was totally always going to. "Oh well, okay. If you insist." He shoved one in his mouth. "Mmm, good." He swallowed that down and took a second one. "You guys have a good night."

He waved me off, and I shut the door behind him. Lawson looked a little uncomfortable. "Are we in trouble?"

"No," I said with a chuckle. "Though it's almost midnight."

"Oh, I hadn't realised it was so late," he said, standing up. He started to clear up. "What do we do with our plates?"

"Here, let me," I said, piling the plates into the basket on the table. "I'll take it all home and wash it." I packed it all away, empty bottles, vase and all, and when the small bakery was back to normal, I opened the door and waited for Lawson to walk out before pulling the door locked shut behind me. He stopped at my ute, and when I put the basket in the back, he lifted the single daisy from the vase. He didn't say a word, just gave me a shy smile, then climbed into the passenger seat holding the flower between his long, thin fingers.

I jumped in behind the wheel and started the ute. It was only a short drive to where he was staying, so I didn't have time to waste. "So, what are you actually doing in Scottsdale? I know you don't want to talk about what the professor told you, but am I allowed to know at least how long you'll be in town for?"

He bit his bottom lip. "I'll be here for a week."

"Seven days, huh?" I couldn't help but smile. "Then there's a good chance I'll see you again?"

"I should expect so," he said simply. "I'll be at the Parks and Wildlife office in the morning to collect my visitor permits. After I sort out the rental car fiasco, that is."

A slow smile spread across my face. "Visitor permits?"

"Yes. Professor Tillman organised it during the week. When you were in Melbourne, I suspect. I'll be surveying *Lepidoptera* in Mount Stronach Forest Reserve for the week. I would think there's a good chance you'll be seeing quite a bit of me in the next seven days."

I pulled up out the front of the B&B and killed the engine. I had to bite my bottom lip to stop from grinning. This was possibly the best news I'd ever heard. "Mount Stronach?"

"Yes. Have you heard of it?"

"Heard of it? That's my jurisdiction. I mean, it's one of the national parks I look after. I know it well."

"I assumed it might be," he said. "Well, I hoped. It would mean a greater chance of seeing you again." He looked at the flower he was holding and chewed on his bottom lip. "If you don't mind me saying that."

"I don't mind at all."

In the low light of the night, he looked even more pale, more beautiful. He held up the flower and stared right at me. "Thank you for the daisy. And thank you for such a lovely evening."

The air between us was suddenly electric. God, I wanted so bad to kiss him, not sure how I should proceed. There was the console of the ute between us, and if I leaned in and he didn't, I'd die of embarrassment...

He licked his lips. "I believe it's customary for a gentleman to offer a kiss on a first date."

I barked out a laugh, thankful, relieved. "I believe it is too," I murmured. I leaned across and slid my hand along his cheek, gently bringing his lips to mine. Soft, warm, sweet, and with the barest hint of parted lips and the promise to deepen but not yet...

Perfect.

Lawson's eyelids fluttered when I pulled back, and he blushed with a smile that stole my breath. "Tomorrow," he whispered.

I nodded, not trusting my voice.

He got out and disappeared into the darkness, and I drove home in a daze. I was grinning like crazy and unable to stop it. I slid the basket of dirty plates on the sink to leave until morning, gave Rosemary a pat and apologised for waking her, and for leaving her all week with Remmy, and then again leaving her tonight. She looked up at me with her big brown Border collie eyes, probably wondering what on earth made me so damn happy at half-past twelve in the morning.

"I met someone special today," I told her. "His name is Lawson Gale." She wagged her tail at me. "I dunno, Rosie, but if there's any such thing as perfect for me, he just might be it."

* * *

At ten o'clock, after I'd been at work for three hours watching the door in case he turned up, Perfect walked in. Well, not so much as *walked in* as kind of *tripped through* the doors, trying to hold a folder in one hand, hold a phone to his ear with his other hand, while opening the door with his elbow. He almost dropped the folder, managed to catch it, but caught his foot on the threshold.

He stumbled a little but thankfully didn't fall over. He collected himself and raised his chin defiantly. "I'll be in touch," he said into the phone. He disconnected the call and, looking around the office, found me smiling at him.

God, he was just even better looking today than he was yesterday. He was wearing navy chinos and a white button-down shirt. His sleeves were rolled halfway up his forearms and his top button was undone. The hollow of his throat looked inviting and I wanted to lick it. "Good morning."

His cheeks tinted a faint pink. "Well, yes. It is now. I suppose. The car rental company finally found my paperwork. It only took them two hours this morning, and I only had to yell a few times." He slid his folder onto the reception counter and took a deep breath. "Sorry. It's been quite a morning."

"Did you get a car sorted out, though?"

"Yes, thank you. A rather big one. I'm not entirely sure what exactly the design team was overcompensating for when they came up with it."

I looked out the window and saw the latest model white Land Rover Defender parked out the front. I smiled at his overcompensating comment. "You'll need the torque if you're going off-road, particularly in the mountains around here."

"Yes, well, true. Not that I'll be going anywhere too dangerous." He looked horrified at the thought. "Well, I don't think I am. Topographical maps can be deceiving."

"Have you got a map of where you're required to go specifically?" I asked. I'd gone through the application this morning, so I knew where he was going. I wanted to know if he did.

"Yes." He pulled out a paper map, then a tablet, and showed me the areas on both. He was familiar with where he had to go, hypothetically anyway. In a physical sense, I wasn't so sure. Yes, he was smart, but wandering off into the Tasmanian wilds on your own was nothing to be blasé about.

"Do you need someone to go with you?"

"I'm not stupid."

I smiled at his indignant rebuff. Always on the defensive. "I never said you were. In fact, we both know you're the opposite of stupid. This area through here"—I pointed to the part of the map he was wanting to go—"isn't easy to access. There's a gorge that runs right along here. But there's a fire trail that runs across the bluff. I can get you access to it if you want."

"Oh." He blinked a few times, and I could almost hear the cogs turning behind his eyes. "Would the person who comes with me require payment? Are they talkers? Because if they don't shut up, I'd rather get lost in the forest by myself." I chuckled at that, which he ignored. "I'm not saying I can't make my own way, but I would not be opposed to guided help, even if just for the first day."

He was so adorable. I could see why his co-workers probably didn't exactly like his brashness, but I found it endearing. He didn't mean any harm by what he said or how he said it. He simply said what he thought because it made sense to him, and it was very clear he compartmentalised; emotions and ego were not mutually exclusive with his work.

"I don't doubt your competence or ability," I said with a smile. "I was referring to a personal guide, a Parks and Wildlife Officer, to be exact."

He stared at me blankly. Okay, so genius, maybe. Clueless, definitely. "That would be me."

"*Oh.*" He looked around the office again. "Are you not busy? Is the office always empty? I would have assumed for a government agency you'd put our taxes to better use."

I scoffed and put my hand to my heart. "You wound me! Robert is at a careers day at the high school, which I cheerfully let him do—"

"Let him or made him?"

"*Made* is a strong word. It was more a case of rock, paper, scissors."

"Who is Robert?"

"He's my 2IC." I waved at the desk on the right. "That's his desk and that one's mine." I pointed to the other desk. "And this one here"—I waved to the front desk—"belongs to Karen, our wonderful office manager who keeps us all organised. She has just ducked down to the coffee shop to get us both a brew. I need some extra help staying awake because someone kept me up talking half the night, and I was here early because I had no clue what time he'd drop by and I didn't want to miss him. I really should have grabbed his phone number."

He chuckled. "Well, if you're offering to be my guide and you can spare the hours, I would happily agree."

"Ah, but it's a no to a phone number."

Lawson fished his mobile out of his pocket and handed it to me. "If you would be so kind as to add your number as a contact." I did as he asked and handed it straight back to him. He held it up and hit Call, making my mobile ring on my desk. "You now have my number."

Just then, the door opened and Karen walked in carrying a takeaway tray with two coffees. "Oh, hello there," she said cheerfully, as always. She handed me a cup. "For you."

"Karen, this is Lawson Gale. The Mount Stronach permit is for him. In fact, I'll be showing him the area today. I'll be back by five."

"Okay," Karen said, sipping her coffee. She looked at Lawson. "Nice to meet you."

He smiled politely. "Nice to meet you too."

I grabbed my phone, keys, and a handful of files, and Lawson collected his folder. I stopped at my ute. "Have you got a medical kit?" I asked him.

"Yes, of course." Lawson opened the rear door in his rented Defender. Inside were eight plastic tubs, some empty, some filled with papers and jars, and a white box with a very discernible medical cross.

I was surprised, to say the least. "Did you have these packed in your suitcase?"

"No. I had them sent ahead."

"What exactly are you doing out in Stronach? I assume it has something to do with whatever your professor asked to see you about?"

"You would assume correctly." Lawson held out the car keys. "Are you driving?"

"No. Guide only. That way you'll be familiar when you drive out by yourself."

We headed down the Tasman Highway for a while, and at my instruction, we turned off at the rifle range road. After about ten kilometres, the road thinned out and became more of a track. It was bumpy and jarring, but at least the scenery was lovely. Lawson knocked the gears back to second to navigate a steep incline. "Does this billygoat track actually lead anywhere? Or are you taking me to your favourite serial killer spot?"

I laughed at him. "You know, you actually handle a four-wheel drive vehicle pretty good. I'm impressed."

"No. You're surprised. Why would you assume I can't drive?"

"I don't really know."

"You thought I was just a lab rat who never takes off his white coat."

"Do you wear a white coat?" I asked, waggling my eyebrows.

He laughed at that. "Wouldn't you like to know?"

"Yes, I would. That's why I asked. I also asked what you were doing out here in the middle of the forest at the instruction of a retired professor, but you didn't answer that either." I pointed up ahead to a turn-off, which was more of a track than the track we were on. "The clearing you're after will be up ahead, about two hundred metres."

Lawson navigated the Defender easily and pulled up in the clearing. "What Professor Tillman asked me to look for is a specimen of *Copper Lycaenidae*."

"I'm going to assume that's a type of butterfly."

He cut the engine. "Yes, it is."

"He called you to come here, all the way from Melbourne, to look for a butterfly?"

"Yes, he did."

"What's so special about it?"

Lawson hopped out of the Defender, turned back, and grinned at me. "It doesn't exist."

# CHAPTER SIX

## *Lawson*

The Tasmanian summer was hot and dry. Not as hot as Melbourne, but still, I hadn't expected it to be this warm. I opened the back door of the Defender and pulled out one of the plastic tubs. Jack was suddenly beside me. "What do you mean, it doesn't exist?"

I handed him the tub. "As in, non-existent. Never been documented."

"How is that possible?" he asked, looking at the tub, then back at me. "I mean, if it doesn't exist, how can you look for it? How can you even know to look for it?"

I stacked another tub on top of the first one Jack was holding. "Well, you see, Professor Tillman believes they're here."

He looked around the woodlands, but the look on his face had sceptical written all over it. "He believes they're here?"

"Correct."

I stacked two tubs on top of each other and lifted them out of the Defender and walked out into the clearing. "Boy, it's warm. I thought Tasmania was supposed to be cold."

Jack followed me. "It is. Normally. I mean, down south it gets cold, but up here it's not too bad. We're in a drought, remember? That generally means dry. Not forgetting the fact it's summer."

I stopped walking and looked right at him. "Are you being facetious?"

He grinned. "Facetious is a little harsh. I think roguish is more flattering, possibly with a dash of sarcasm."

"I'm not a fan of sarcasm."

"Then why are you smiling?"

"Because I do happen to like roguish."

We stood facing each other, both holding two tubs each, both smiling. "What's in the boxes?" he asked eventually.

"My equipment."

Jack's lips twitched. "Your equipment? Really?"

I rolled my eyes and put the tubs on the ground. "My field equipment. I have a backpack, notebooks, texts, notes, specimen jars. A GPS, emergency beacon, thermometer, barometer, satellite phone." Jack's smile got wider when I listed each item. "What?"

He put the tubs he was holding down next to mine. "I dunno. I don't know what I was expecting." He was still smiling but it was as though he was secretly pleased. "You have all the right gear."

"Well, of course I do."

"Most academic types come out with no supplies, no tracking equipment, and no clue, if I'm being honest."

"Did you assume me to be irresponsible?"

Jack seemed to consider his answer before speaking. "Let's just say I had my concerns, but I'm pleasantly surprised."

"I spent many vacations and weekends in national parks in and around Melbourne as a child and was taught the importance of safety from the very first. As I grew older, particularly now, I do a lot of field study alone. Like when I was in the middle of the Blue Mountains by myself, I was very aware of my isolation."

"Do you always do field study by yourself?"

"Mostly." I shrugged. "I love it. I'm comfortable with my own company enough to spend hours, or days, by myself."

Jack frowned. "Are you bothered by my being here?"

"Not at all. Though I do have work to do."

"Right." He took a step back, fighting a smile. "Then I'll let you do... whatever it is you do when you look for a butterfly that doesn't exist." He took a few more steps backwards, smiling now, before he turned and walked back to the Defender.

Jack Brighton really was a very good looking man, and the playfulness and flirting were exhilarating. The anticipation even more so. I would be very interested in something physical happening between us, and I had no issue in instigating it if I had to. But now was not the time. Professor Tillman had entrusted me with what could be the legacy of his career.

He swore to me the species was here. He'd seen it. Many years ago when he had youth on his side, a keen mind and able body, he'd hiked all over these ranges. It was the late seventies, he'd said. He had no paper or pencil and his camera was out of film. He'd seen one single specimen. That was all. He'd gone home and drawn what he saw from memory, and he'd been back a hundred times in the years that followed. But he'd never seen it again.

Now his mind was still keen but his body wasn't able. He told me he'd met a lot of lepidopterists over the decades, but none that he trusted. Until me.

In his words, I wasn't owned by The Society. Yes, I worked under the world-renowned Professor Michael Asterly at Melbourne University. Yes, I was his best and brightest student: I published journal articles years before my classmates, and yes, I was one of the best. It wasn't even that I'd specialised in *Lycaenidae*. It was because I wasn't liked by the *scholar squad*, he'd called them. And that, according to Professor Tillman was why he chose me. As it turned out, he never cared much for their opinions either.

When he'd told them he'd seen an Eltham Copper Butterfly in Tasmania, they'd laughed at him. Only it wasn't an Eltham Copper. How could it be when it was not found anywhere near Eltham? Eltham Coppers were so named, they reminded him, because Eltham, Victoria, was the only area in which they were found. But Professor Tillman was adamant. He said it was *like* an Eltham Copper though it had varying distinct marks on its hindwing, like no other Copper in any book he'd found. And that made it a new discovery. A new species.

But he had no proof. And after decades of fruitless searching, he'd passed the baton onto me.

So, with that in mind, I opened the first tub and got to work.

I took recordings of temperature, wind direction, GPS location, aspect, and sun position. Then I took notes on plant types and soil types. I could see why the professor had liked this area for finding Coppers. On paper, it was perfect.

Eltham Coppers liked north facing aspect for warmer weather, they lived in vegetation classified as woodland, and this area was both of those things. If I were a betting man and these butterflies were going to be found in an area outside of Victoria, then I'd say there was a very good chance for it to be here.

I got so carried away with my data collation like I always do, that I forgot Jack was in the Defender. Actually, I kind of forgot he was there at all.

"Hey!" his voice, even far off, still alarmed me.

I spun to the sound of it, to find him trudging through the scrub toward me. "Jeez, you scared me," I admitted with my hand to my heart.

It took him a few seconds to keep walking so he was close enough for a conversation. "You always make a habit of walking off without telling someone where you're going?"

"Well, no. I'm normally here by myself," I explained. I pulled the GPS and satellite phone from my backpack. "I know where I am."

"Yeah, but I didn't know. I finished my paperwork, looked up, and you were gone."

"Oh."

"Scared the crap outta me."

"Sorry." I felt bad about making him worry. "How did you find me?"

He finally smiled. "You were whistling. A tune or something."

"Was I?" I had been told by other colleagues that I tended to whistle to myself when I was lost in my work, particularly out in the field. "I didn't realise."

"Lucky you hadn't gone too far or I wouldn't have heard you." Jack gave a nod back to the direction he'd come, and following his line of sight, I could just make out the white of the Defender through the scrub. "Found anything yet?"

"Not yet. It's mostly data collation at this stage. The conditions are right, though. The elements and vegetation are correct for the habitat of Coppers, though I've not seen any ant colonies or any butterflies, for that matter."

"What do they look like?" he asked. "I mean, I could've seen one by now and wouldn't have known."

"Have you ever paid attention to butterflies?"

His lip pulled down to one corner. "Well, no. Not really."

From my pocket I fished out the photocopy of the professor's drawing and showed it to him. "That's it."

It was a detailed sketch, the very one the professor had drawn all those decades ago. The copper-coloured wings were what gave the specimen its name.

Jack looked from the drawing to me. "It's brown."

"That's a photocopy of an old drawing. The butterfly is copper. Hence the name Eltham Copper."

"Okay, so it's not brown. It's copper." I was surprised he didn't roll his eyes.

"Coppers are part of the *Lycaenidae* genus, and Elthams, in particular are on the endangered species list. I happen to study them in efforts of conservation."

"Endangered?"

"Yes. They're found in only a few very small, decreasing pockets of vegetation in Victoria. So I'm sure you can appreciate the importance of what the professor found."

Jack nodded, all humour gone. "Yes, of course. I didn't realise it was endangered." He seemed to think something over in his mind for a moment. "How do you go about finding them? I mean, it's not like animal tracks. The Tasmanian devils, for example, dig burrows, leave scratch marks on trees and logs, and disturb the topsoil. Or there's leftover meals or scat. Actually, they're messy buggers. Butterflies aren't exactly intrusive."

It was a good question, and one I got asked frequently. "There are markers, if you know what to look for. The Eltham Copper have a very complex triangular dependency with the *Notoncus* ant and the *Bursaria spinosa*—"

"Sweet Bursaria? The shrub?"

"Yes. Are you familiar with it?"

"Well, yeah. It grows all over these ranges."

Flora and fauna, of course. I started to smile. "Can you identify more specific areas on my map?"

"Sure I can. It's my job."

I leaned up on my toes and kissed him softly on the lips. "You are a godsend."

He grinned. I had no idea one little kiss could make him smile like that. "Maybe we could go over all your maps tonight with dinner?"

"You've set the bar pretty high for date expectations," I teased. "Not sure what you could do to beat last night."

"I'll think of something."

"Then I'd love to."

He leaned in and, with his fingers under my chin, tilted my face up toward his. He pressed his lips to mine, gently at first, then harder, and sliding his hand along my jaw, he urged my lips open with his own. God, how he kissed me.

In that perfect moment, the world stopped turning. Nothing existed but him. He left me breathless and dizzy, and certain of one thing.

There was more on the menu tonight than just dinner.

# CHAPTER SEVEN

## *Jack*

I couldn't help myself. I *had* to kiss him. Well, technically, he put kissing on the table first. Albeit, his was a chaste kiss, but it was still a kiss. And I'd never been one to do things by halves. If I was gonna kiss him and kiss him properly, then it'd be a kiss he'd remember.

And holy shit, what a kiss it was.

When I pulled away, his eyes were unfocused and his lips were red and wet. We were both breathless, but this was different.

He took my damn breath away. "You are sublime."

"Oh." He blushed, and the colour that crossed his cheeks matched the delicious colour of his lips. "No one's ever called me that before."

I ran my thumb across his cheek. "Then they were fools."

Lawson bit his lip. His shyness was charming in a way I'd never fancied before. Normally I'd go for guys who were more a physical match to me—masculine with more brawn than brains—but there was something about this butterfly-chasing genius that really drew me in.

He let out a little chuckle and stepped back, apparently so he could take a few breaths. "Okay, so I seem to have some kind of cognitive dysfunction when you're too close."

I laughed. "Sounds serious."

He put his hand to his forehead, and I might have been worried if he wasn't smiling. "Could be." Then he looked up to the sky. "Should we be heading back?"

I checked my watch. "Probably. It's just after four."

43

We walked back toward the clearing. Lawson packed everything away neatly into the tubs, and we loaded them into the Defender and headed back to town. He drove for a while, then he asked, "So, what are you planning for our date tonight? Because if we're heading back into Launceston, I'll need some time to transfer my data to my laptop."

"Did you want to head back into Launceston?"

"Well, no. Not really. As nice as a fancy dinner sounds, I have work to do."

"What makes you think I can't get you a fancy dinner in Scottsdale?"

"Well, the table for two in the bakery is going to be hard to beat."

I grinned at him. "Mr Gale, that sounds like a challenge."

He made a happy sound. "I believe it was supposed to. I have high expectations, remember?"

"How can I forget?" I took his GPS from his dash.

"What are you doing?"

"Adding in the address you'll need to get to for the best date ever." I put the GPS back into its dash holder. "Bring whatever work you want to go over too."

"Are you sure?" He looked from the road to me and back to the road. "Not to say I'm not grateful for the offer. But working on a date?"

I looked out the window and tried to play it cool. "Well, you're only here for a week, so the work you're doing is not only important, but you're also on a very limited schedule. If we have to multitask, that's okay with me."

He looked at me again for a long second before turning his attention back to driving. "Thank you. For saying that."

"What? That multitasking is okay?"

"No. For saying my work is important."

"Environmental conservation of any kind is important."

Lawson smiled. "You know, it's already highly likely you'll get lucky to some degree tonight. You don't have to butter me up."

I laughed at that. "Can't say I've ever used dairy spread as a personal lubricant, but I'm not opposed to trying."

His mouth fell open and he stared at me, as though he was half-amused, half-horrified.

"Please watch the road," I said, pointing to the windscreen. "We can't have the best second date ever if we die in a car crash."

* * *

I heard the Defender pull up out the front of my place and watched Lawson get out. I think it took him a second to realise he was at my house. It was, after all, the address I'd given him. He appeared hesitant to walk up to the garden gate, so I opened the front door. He wore the same navy trousers but had changed his shirt. This one was a short-sleeve button-down with some triangle pattern. And sweet mother of God, he was wearing a bow tie. I had to steady my breath before I could speak. "Hey. You look lost."

He patted down his already perfectly combed hair. "Well, I wasn't expecting… actually, I didn't know what to expect. The address you gave me was out of town, and this is the only house for miles… Then I saw your work ute."

I walked out to meet him, and I could see he was taking in the view. There were mountains to the north-east, a valley to the west. I lived in a tidy three-bedroom timber cottage painted pale yellow with white trim on the veranda that wrapped around all sides of the house. It was old but had character. The best part was, the cottage was on a ten-acre lot in the middle of larger properties, which meant there were no other houses in sight. "So, uh, this is my house."

He smiled up at me. "It's very quaint." He listened for a second. "And very quiet."

"Which is why I love it." I leaned in and gave him a soft kiss on the lips. "Thank you for coming."

He sighed happily before turning back to his rental. "Can you help me carry these?"

I had no idea what *these* were. "Sure."

He opened the back door to the Defender and pulled out one of the tubs he'd had in the clearing earlier today and handed it to me. He grabbed a laptop bag and held it to his chest. "Something smells really good."

"Dinner or the jasmine? Or me? Because I did have a shower."

He smiled at that. "I was referring to the food. The jasmine plant is nice, though. And I haven't smelled you." He paused for a moment. "Yet." Then he looked around me and nodded to the front door. "Are you going to invite me inside, or are we dining out here tonight?"

"Oh, yes, of course," I said, walking down the path to my front veranda. "Someone's very excited to meet you."

"Oh," he mumbled. I stopped on the steps and turned to him. He looked put off and a little confused. "I wasn't expecting there to be anyone else here."

I smiled at him. "Her name is Rosemary. She promised to be on her best behaviour." I crossed the veranda and opened the door. Rosemary was still sitting like a very good girl where I'd told her to stay. "Come." She padded over to me, then stuck her head out the door behind my legs. "Rosemary, I'd like you to meet Lawson."

How this meeting went was critical for me. If she didn't like him, or if he wasn't a dog person, I'd be very disappointed. It would mean that whatever was starting between Lawson and me would end tonight. I couldn't have a man in my life who didn't accept Rosemary into his. Me and my dog were a package deal.

I was nervous because I really wanted this to go well. I liked Lawson, and I really thought we had a connection, a beginning of something that could be very special. Permanent even, if it was possible to know that after just a few short days. But their getting along was the catalyst on where we went from here.

My worries went unfounded because Lawson broke out in a grin when he saw her, and my dog immediately wagged her tail. She went out to meet him, and Lawson put his laptop bag on the ground, bent down on my one knee, and gave her a good, hearty pat.

The relief and happiness that went through me were unprecedented.

He didn't just say 'oh cute dog' and walk past her. He stopped, put down his bag, and met her on her level. Rosemary gave me a tongue-lolling grin as he ruffled her fur, which was all the approval I needed.

Lawson stood up and brushed off his knee, then looked at me and grinned. "She's gorgeous."

I was pretty sure my smile was about to break my face. "She is." I couldn't help myself. I walked back across the veranda, down the steps to where he stood. I held the storage tub on my hip with my left hand and used my right hand to tilt his face up so I could press my lips to his. Soft and warm, lingering for a moment. "And so are you."

His cheeks coloured and he ducked his head. Even the tips of his ears went red. It did all sorts of wonderful things to my stomach. It stirred even better things in my groin. "I better check on dinner." My voice was gruff so I cleared my throat. "Please, come inside."

Lawson followed me in. My house wasn't anything fancy or big. The living area consisted of one room that was my lounge room at the front, dining room at the back, kitchen at the side. There was a doorway off the lounge room that became a short hall for three bedrooms, one bathroom, and a laundry. It had timber floors, pale yellow walls, and the kitchen was kinda old. I guessed the decorating types these days would call it retro or country chic. Rosemary trotted over to her bed in front of the unlit fire and lay down.

I headed straight for the kitchen, sliding the plastic tub onto the far end of the dining table on my way. Lawson put his laptop next to it and stood at the kitchen counter. He eyed off where I'd set the end of the table for two, wine glasses and candle included. He smiled. "You have a lovely home."

I collected the tea towel off the kitchen bench and gave him a quick smile. "Thanks. It's old, but she's got that old-home charm. I love it." I opened the oven door and took out the dish of bubbling lasagne. I carefully slid it onto the stove top so it could cool a bit. "I hope you like lasagne and salad."

"Perfect. And homemade? I'm impressed."

"So, the second date might live up to the first yet!"

He chuckled. "It's off to a very good start. Though I'll let you know my full assessment when I leave."

It was hard to tell if he was joking because he smirked when he said it, but knowing him, I fully expected him to tell me what I did right *and* wrong. "If there was going to be a test, I would've made dessert."

He looked right into my eyes, almost daring in a way. "I'm sure you can improvise."

He wasn't talking about food.

It made my heart skip a beat and sent a warm thrill through my balls. "I'm sure I can."

He licked his lips and smiled. "So? Should we look over the maps before or after dinner?"

"After."

I took the green leafy salad from the fridge, uncovered it, and spritzed it with dressing before dishing up a decent square of lasagne onto two plates. He carried them to the table, I carried the salad, then grabbed the bottle of red wine I'd bought on my way home, and set it between our plates. I pulled out Lawson's seat and lit the candle while he sat down and got comfortable. "This is very lovely," he said.

"Thank you." Using the tongs, I scooped out a portion of salad onto his plate, then mine, and then poured his wine first. "Did you get everything done you wanted to this afternoon? You were transferring something to your laptop?"

"Yes. I know most people detest data entry, but I don't mind," he said. He took a small mouthful of lasagne and chewed and swallowed appreciatively. "This is very good."

"It's my Nonna's recipe."

"Nonna?" he asked. "Is your family Italian?"

"On my mum's side. My dad's side came here with the convicts."

Lawson smiled and sipped his wine. "My family's about five generations Australian. Before that we came from England and Ireland." He ate another forkful of lasagne and hummed as he swallowed it down. "Tell me about Rosemary."

"She's almost three. I got her when she was about eight weeks old. Full of mischief but the brightest eyes you've ever seen. Smart as a whip. Smarter than me, anyhow."

"And her name?" he asked. "Rosemary isn't a very common name for a dog."

I had to finish my mouthful before I could speak. "There's a thicket of rosemary that runs down the side of the house. The day I brought her home, she ran straight for it and I couldn't get her out of it. She'd roll in it, lay in it, chew it. And I couldn't pick a name for her, but every time anyone would pick her up, they'd say, 'oh, rosemary,' so it kinda stuck."

He smiled as I told my story, then nodded over to where she was asleep in her bed. "She's very spoilt."

"One hundred per cent," I agreed. "She normally comes out into the field with me. If I have a day where I'm out and about in the national parks, she's usually sitting right up beside me. If I hadda known we were gonna be out all day, I would've brought her along."

"Next time then."

"Will there be a next time?" My heart stopped while I waited for his answer.

"Do you not have work to do?" he asked, but he smiled as he spoke.

"Of course. But like I said, helping out on a conservation study is work-related. If you're busy doing your thing, I can do my own reports and data collation when I'm out. Take photos of vegetation, soil reports, water levels, check on some known animal habitats, check fencing, that kind of thing."

"Okay." He nodded. "I'd like that very much."

Again with the belly somersault. "Me too."

We ate our dinner, of which Lawson devoured everything in front of him. When his plate was clean, he leaned back and patted his stomach. "Wow. Compliments to the chef and to your Nonna. That was delicious."

I grinned proudly. "Secret is in the ricotta."

"I look forward to seeing what you can do for Date Number Three."

I raised an eyebrow at him but could feel the smile spreading on my face. "I thought you were waiting until you were leaving for your full assessment."

He rolled his eyes. "I think we both know there will be another one. I wouldn't mind seeing Rosemary again."

I scoffed. "Thank you very much. I'll never doubt where your affection lies again."

He chuckled, then sipped his wine. "So tell me, why are you single?"

Right. Straight to the point.

He narrowed his eyes at me. "You are single, aren't you? Because the likelihood of a third date balances precariously on your answer."

"I am most definitely single," I answered. "As to why... well, the last guy I was seeing lived in Hobart, and the commute didn't work for him."

"Oh."

"And the guy before that lasted only two dates. The first date, we had dinner in Launceston. That went okay. Second date, I invited him here. He got as far as the gate before Rosemary started to growl. That was the end of that."

"Dogs are outstanding judges of character."

"They are. I'd trust her judgement before any human I know."

"She likes me." Then he tilted his head. "Was asking me here some kind of test?"

I laughed. "Yes. And you passed with flying colours."

He seemed put out for half a second before the smile he was fighting won out. He sipped his wine, and I did the same. "And commuting or any kind of long distance relationships are out?"

So I wasn't alone in thinking this could be the start of something... Yes, we lived in different states but were most definitely on the same page. I put my wine glass on the table and met his gaze. "For him it was. Not me."

"Good." He nodded slowly before giving me that shy smile that belied his forthright nature. He stood up and collected our plates. "Let's get this cleaned up, then we pull those maps out."

Twenty minutes later, the kitchen was sparkling, a second glass each of wine was poured, and a large map was unfolded, spread out on the dining table. "If you mark on there, I can transfer it to this," Lawson said, showing me the exact same map on his laptop. "I prefer to have both. There's no saying my laptop will work when I'm hours from anywhere, so it's best to have it on both. Particularly for safety reasons."

"Smart," I said with a nod. "Especially if you go out by yourself, like you said you were prone to do."

"I always leave a detailed map of where I'm going with my professor or colleagues if I go solo." He shrugged one shoulder. "I'd be loath for the news headline to read 'Genius is an idiot who gets lost'."

I laughed at that, then showed him the vegetation maps Parks and Wildlife Services had, outlining documented locations of the particular plant he was after. I transferred the info onto his paper map, and he did the digital. Then I added in the locations I'd seen it personally, paying particular attention to the factors he said were important to his species of butterfly. North facing aspect, warmer climes.

Lawson pointed out the area he intended on searching in the morning and wrote down the GPS locations in his online journal. I really admired how meticulous he was. He was particular about the details, and that probably annoyed some people. But not me.

He was standing, leaning over his laptop, and I was standing beside him, where I'd been studying the unfolded map. I looked at him instead. "Still want me to join you tomorrow?"

He stood up straight and turned to face me. I wasn't aware of how close we were until then. Until he looked up at me and I could see the flecks of gold in the blue of his eyes and how long his eyelashes were. His skin was perfect in its paleness, his lips looked redder than I remembered.

"I'd very much like to kiss you right now," he mumbled.

I wasn't sure if he'd meant to say that out loud, but it was like he read my mind. I cupped my hand to his jaw. "I was just thinking the same thing."

"I can tell," he whispered. "You look at my mouth—"

I covered his lips with my own, and he eagerly met my kiss. God, he tasted so good. He felt even better. Lawson wrapped one arm around me and slid his other hand through my hair and slipped his tongue into my mouth. It almost buckled my knees.

I groaned into his kiss and pulled him against me. He came willingly, melting into my arms. He gave himself to me in that moment. In that kiss. He was putty in my hands, and I wanted to mould him, I wanted to take him, claim and make him mine.

All this from just a kiss. My world had tilted on its axis, nothing would ever be the same again.

From just one kiss.

Lawson hummed before pulling back a little. I cupped his face in my two hands and fluttered my eyelashes against his cheek.

"What are you doing?" he whispered.

"Butterfly kisses," I murmured before pressing my lips to his once more.

His eyes danced with something like happiness, but just when I thought he was going to say he should go, he surprised me yet again.

I should know better than to expect anything but the unexpected.

# CHAPTER EIGHT

## *Lawson*

I wasn't normally so brazen to suggest such things outright, but I couldn't help myself. I wasn't ready for this to end right now; I needed more of him. And from the way he kissed me, I was certain he felt the same.

"I think we should move to somewhere more comfortable."

I took his hand and pulled him toward the couch. I didn't think the bedroom was strictly appropriate. Not yet, anyway. I stopped in front of the sofa, and Jack's nostrils flared. He licked his lips, and sliding his hand around my neck, he crushed his mouth to mine hard enough to push me backwards. His other arm wrapped around my back, and he lowered me onto the couch.

His strength surprised me. Of course I was aware of his height and his huge shoulders, but he simply manoeuvred me as though I weighed nothing—I was suddenly on my back, lying the length of the sofa and he was over me, caging me in with his arms as he slowly lowered his body onto mine. And it was glorious.

His weight on top of me, between my legs, was heavenly.

He kissed me slower this time, deeper, but with no less passion. Every nerve in my body sang. I rolled my hips, grinding against him, and his breath stuttered as he broke the kiss. "God," he murmured; his voice was rough. He kissed along my jaw to my ear and down my neck. "I want more of your neck, but I really like the bow tie." I could feel him smile against my skin.

I reached up and pulled on one end of my tie, unravelling it, and scrambling to undo the top button. "I don't care much for the bow tie right now," I rasped, tilting my head to give him more of my neck. "Not when you do th—"

Then he scraped his teeth across my skin, and he chuckled as my words stumbled to a stop. But his hot breath down my neck and shoulder sent a shiver right through me, and *that* made Jack moan.

"Lawson," he growled. He pulled back, and his eyes were dark but his smirk was nefarious. "If you keep squirming like that, I won't be responsible for what I do to you."

I laughed and rolled my hips, rubbing my erection against his through the fabric of our clothes. From what I could feel, he was in proportion—to say the least. He was big, and he was hard. I writhed against him again because he felt so incredible. His weight, his hard-on…

Jack's huge hand stilled my hip while he pinned me with his body. "Lawson." There was more warning in his tone now. He began to pull away. "This is about to get embarrassing very fast. You have no idea how much you turn me on."

I hooked my foot around the back of his leg to prevent him from moving. I wanted him right where he was. "This doesn't have to stop," I whispered. I ran my hand down his back, over his arse, and then slowly—so he could deny me if he wished—slid my hand between us and palmed his erection.

Jack whined. He closed his eyes as though he was trying to summon willpower from a higher being.

I'd never felt so empowered. He was half a foot taller than me, outweighed me by twenty kilos, he was athletic and I was academic, yet I was in complete control.

So using both hands, I undid his belt, pulling it roughly through the buckle. Then I popped the button and slid my fingers underneath the elastic of his briefs. His erection was confined toward his hip, so wrapping my hand around him, I pulled his cock free.

His eyes flew open, a mix of lust and abandon stared back at me. "Lawson," he murmured my name before crushing his mouth to mine. I stroked him, gyrating my hips, needing to feel him. Needing more. Needing everything.

Jack pulled back, almost to his haunches, and he undid my trousers. I was transfixed, watching his face as he revealed my cock. He licked his lips and his nostrils flared, and when he gripped my shaft, his eyes met mine, and I just about caught on fire.

"Jack." I don't know what I was insisting on, or begging for. Something. Anything. "Just fucking do it."

His eyes lit up and his smirk was wicked as he aligned our cocks and wrapped his huge hand around us both. I gasped at the onslaught of pleasure, before he kissed me with a fervour I'd never known.

I'd never been wanted like he wanted me.

He broke the kiss and spoke against my lips. "Please come." He groaned, a pained sound. "Need you to come first, and I'm not gonna last."

His hand, now slicked with precome, slid our cocks together, and the feeling was incredible. Knowing I was turning him on so much was dizzying. I looked down between us, my forehead against his neck, and watched as our cockheads squeezed through his hand—it was the most erotic thing I'd ever seen. It was the most erotic thing I'd ever felt, been a part of, or had happen to me. God, I was so turned on. I couldn't ever remember being this aroused…

"Lawson," he growled, pure sex and wonder. "Need you to come."

And I did. A coil, wound so tight, sprung deep at the base of my spine. I came in spurts between us, groaning through an unspeakable pleasure.

"Oh, God," he whispered in my ear, and his cock pulsed against mine as he came. "Fuck!"

Jack held himself above me with one hand, trembling as his orgasm rocketed through him. His face was the picture of ecstasy and bliss. His eyes were heavy-lidded, his lips parted in a silent cry.

Thick ropes of come covered my stomach and shirt. Jack collapsed on top of me, his weight immense and divine, and he nuzzled into my neck. With him in between my thighs, I shifted a little to get more comfortable. He clearly had no intention of moving.

He nuzzled my neck some more, then kissed lazily up my jaw until he found my lips. He rested against his open palm and snugged his elbow in beside my shoulder. He smiled down at me languidly. His eyes were dreamy.

He sighed happily. "We're a mess. I probably should apologise, but I'm not sorry at all."

I bit my bottom lip to stop from smiling too much. Though I doubt I had him fooled. "I probably should apologise for being so bold as to insist you join me on the couch, but I'm not sorry at all either."

He chuckled and planted a soft, wet kiss on my lips. "I do like the way you speak. But I will admit, I like it when you swear even more."

"Swear?"

"You said fuck. Actually, you said 'just fucking do it.'"

"I did not!"

"You did too." He grinned and kissed me again. "And it was hot."

I could feel my cheeks heat. "I'm sure I'm aware of what words come out of my mouth. I'm not one to curse. The English language has many thousand words, some much more indulgent and better serving than swear words."

Now he laughed. "You totally swore. Next time I'll record you so I have proof."

"Next time?"

"Please tell me there'll be a next time."

I found myself smiling at his expression. Blinking innocence and hope. "Will it be the best third date ever?"

"Yes," he answered quickly. "Though, just as a gauge, how did the second date go?"

"I'll let you know when it's over."

He laughed into a sigh and smiled as though he couldn't possibly have been happier. "I think you should stay the night."

Oh. My heart squeezed with his words and the look in his eyes. "Well, no. I think I shouldn't. I appreciate the offer, but I have none of my belongings here and I have an early start tomorrow."

"Am I not coming with you tomorrow?"

"If you want."

"I want. You, me, and Rosemary. I thought we had a deal?"

I looked over to find her still sound asleep in front of the unlit fireplace, then back to Jack. "Okay, deal."

"So you'll stay?"

I smiled at his insistence. "No."

He pouted gorgeously. "Then I better make Date Number Three even better."

"Or even Date Number Four…"

He kissed me with smiling lips. "I'm not afraid of working for it."

"It? As in sex? You presume a lot."

"I wasn't referring to working for sex, no. I was referring to working on making you happier with each date." He seemed amused. "If more sex is a reward for awesome date planning, then I'm not opposed. And I'm not presuming anything. I seem to recall you dragging me to the couch to get more comfortable."

I'm certain I blushed. "I believe in asking for what I want. There's no point in yearning for something if you can actually have it."

Jack traced his thumb over my heated cheek. His eyes followed his thumb, then scanned my face. "You are

58

something special," he whispered. "And you can have me anytime you want me."

I leaned up and kissed him. "I think I need to get cleaned up."

He jumped off me with the agility of a cat and walked off down the hall. "Take off your shirt. I'll get you a clean one."

I pulled at the unravelled bow tie, sliding it from around my neck, then undid the buttons on my shirt. I slid it from my shoulders just as Jack came back with a wet washer in one hand and a folded shirt in the other. And he stopped. And stared.

I felt warm all over as he examined me with his gaze, as though his eyes were hands that skimmed over every inch of my skin.

Jack licked his lips and took a robotic step toward me. "Oh wow," he said, now appearing to be fixated on my chest. He swallowed hard and finally met my eyes. "Right, then. Shirt?" He held up his hand with the shirt. "Though I'll be completely honest with you, Lawson, I'd rather you didn't put it on."

He stood in front of me; his height and size never seemed more apparent. I felt slightly vulnerable, I was half-naked and he towered over me, his shoulders dwarfed mine. But he very tenderly put the washcloth to my abdomen, gently washing me clean in slow, deliberate circles.

It was the most adoring, indulgent thing anyone had ever done for me.

He pressed a kiss to the top of my shoulder, and I almost told him I was staying…

Jack took a small step backward and let out a slow breath. "A shirt," he said, his voice low and lovely. "It will be too big, but it's the smallest I've got. I haven't worn it in years."

I took the folded shirt. "Thank you." I slipped it on over my head, and yes, it swam on me.

When I finished pressing it down into submission, I looked up at Jack to find him biting the corner of his bottom lip. "Looks good on you."

"It's far too big." I tried tucking the front in a bit, but it was pointless.

Jack put his fingers under my chin and gently tipped my face upwards so I would look at him. "I like my clothes on you," he murmured before pressing his lips to mine.

I slid my hand along his jaw, the feel of stubble scratched my skin in the most delicious way, and I deepened the kiss. He let me kiss him this way, deep and slick until he put a hand on my hip and pushed me away. He chuckled, a disbelieving sound. His voice was gruff. "If you intend on leaving, you probably should go now. Before I take you to my bed."

I blinked, staring up at him, and somewhere in my brain a voice was telling me to breathe, breathe, because I'd somehow forgotten how to. I took my lungs full of air and my mind buzzed as a response to the reprieve. I put my palm to my forehead, staving off a dizzy spell.

Jack's eyes were a mix of amused and concerned. "You okay?"

"While it's correct that breathing can be both a voluntary and involuntary process, I'm not certain I've ever actually forgotten to breathe before now."

Jack barked out a laugh, and he smiled with a hint of mischief. "You know, if you're feeling lightheaded, you can always stay."

This time, I stepped back. "Thank you for the offer, but I'm fine. Though I really should be going."

He looked disappointed, which made me happier than it should have, but he nodded. "Fair enough. We still on for tomorrow, though?"

"Yes. I'd like that."

"Me too. And I need to put my thinking cap on about Date Number Three. Is tomorrow night too soon?"

I picked up my laptop satchel and smiled at him. "Tomorrow night is fine."

"Good." He collected the storage tub I'd brought with me from the table and followed me to the front door. "I'll wash your shirt for you and leave it here for you then."

I stopped by the light on the front porch and turned to face him. "So, Date Number Three will be here again?"

He blanched and the corner of his lip pulled down with uncertainty. "Well, I thought… we can go somewhere else if you'd prefer. I just thought you could bring your work here and get the paperwork done while I cook dinner, that way we have more time…"

I smiled at him, letting him know it was fine. "Sounds perfect."

He beamed a smile that made my heart soar. Then he ducked his head a little and nodded toward my rental before taking the three porch steps with a familiar ease. He opened the back of the Defender and slid the tub inside. I opened the driver's door and leaned in to put my satchel on the passenger seat. When I straightened up, he was standing behind me and he made no apologies about being caught ogling my arse. I raised my eyebrow at him, but he only shrugged.

"So, do I get a score on tonight's date?" he asked. Then he apparently remembered something out of the blue. "Oh, wait! Hold that thought." He dashed off to the corner of his house, disappearing from the light the front porch allowed. He came back holding a strand of jasmine: dainty white flowers on a sliver of green. He stopped in front of me and presented them to me. There was a nervousness to the set of his lips. "For you. A date's not a date without flowers, apparently."

I reached out slowly and took the flowers. "Perfect."

His smile was my reward. "What's perfect?"

"My assessment on Date Number Two." I took a deep breath and looked up at the amazing blanket of stars above us. The silence, the open space, and seclusion of where he lived was incredible. "I'm starting to think all dates with you might be perfect, varying only in their degree of perfection."

He smiled victoriously, happily. "I'm already looking forward to tomorrow." He put his hand to my face and kissed me. "But if you have to go…"

"I do."

"Then goodnight."

I leaned up and pressed my lips to his. "Goodnight."

He watched as I manoeuvred the ridiculously sized Defender out of his driveway. When I looked back to wave, I saw that Rosemary had joined him on the porch. Jack patted her forehead, said something to her, and waved me off.

I drove back to town with an absurd grin on my face. I went to sleep with it too.

# CHAPTER NINE

## *Jack*

I pushed the door to the bakery open, welcomed by the ding of the bell above the door, then by Remmy. "Oh hey, you! You're in early!" Then she eyed me cautiously. "Well, look at you."

"What?"

"That smile."

I laughed. "Don't know what you're talking about."

"Oh my God." She walked out from behind the counter, never taking her eyes off me. "It's him, isn't it? The bow tie guy. What was his name? Lawson?"

I pulled my lips into a pout. Well, I tried, but they went back to smiling without my consent. "Yes, his name is Lawson. And I still don't know what you're talking about."

Remmy laughed at me and gave me a hug. "Tell me everything."

"We had a second date last night. Having a third tonight. I'm also spending the day with him out in the national park."

She wrung her hands together and buzzed excitedly. "Did he wear a bow tie last night?"

"Yes, he did."

She made some weird, dramatic sound. "Aww, he's so cute!"

"And he's smart, and he's sexy as hell."

"And Rosemary?"

"Loves him."

Remmy's eyes got teary. "Awwwww."

"Actually, Rosemary is spending the day with us too. I think he's a bit taken with her."

"Thank God. I thought he might be a bit timid around her," Remmy said. "You know, he seemed the type to be timid…"

If she was referring to the nerdy, bow tie-wearing, genius look he had going on, she was very wrong. "Ah, Lawson's not timid." I bit my lip. "About anything."

She laughed and gave me a knowing grin. "And that explains the smile." She went back around the counter. "Did you actually want anything or did you just come in here to brag?"

I snorted. "Surprise me. Anything you think we might like to eat today. And something for Rosemary too."

Remmy had a separate small display of bone shaped cookies for her four-legged customers. Made solely with ingredients for human consumption—oats, carrot, peanut butter, honey—Rosemary would eat them as fast as Remmy could make them.

Remmy put some pastries and bread into a paper bag for me. "What are your plans for your date tonight?"

"Not sure yet. Something at home. I'll cook for him again while he gets through his paperwork, which will leave more time for… other things."

"Ah, confident, I see?"

"Well, I don't think I should assume anything when it comes to Lawson. I get the feeling he'll keep me on my toes." I was back to smiling. "In a good way, of course."

Remmy winked. "Of course."

"Well, I better get going." I took the bag of goods and offered her a twenty, which she refused to take. So, without a word, I walked around her side of the counter, opened the till, and slid the money inside. She rolled her eyes. I gave her a kiss on the cheek. "Don't want to be late."

"Have fun tonight!" Remmy waved me off as I walked out the door. I put the bag of pastries in the Esky I had on the back of the ute. I'd put some fruit in earlier as well, not knowing what Lawson might want to eat today. I climbed into the driver's seat and gave Rosemary a pat for being patient. "One more stop to make."

I bought some takeaway coffees, enough for everyone in the office and one for Lawson too. I slid the two trays on the floor at the passenger side, where they wouldn't spill onto Rosemary. "Don't touch. They're hot," I told her, though I dunno why. It wasn't like she knew what the word *hot* was. But she knew what *don't touch* was, and like a good girl, she didn't give the trays of coffee a second look. "You'll have to wait until lunchtime for your cookies." Her tongue lolled out in her doggy smile. I was pretty sure she knew what the word cookie was. After me, I think Remmy was her favourite human.

I drove to work, handed out coffees, and explained I'd be out doing field assessments again today. No one batted an eyelid, but when Lawson arrived right on eight thirty, there were a few knowing smiles. No one seemed surprised that Lawson knew Rosemary already, or they hadn't realised that it meant he must have been to my house. But when I walked out the door with him and a tail-wagging Rosemary, Karen gave me a ridiculous smile and mouthed "good luck." I cleared my throat, grateful Lawson hadn't seen it.

The day was warm already. Well, warm for Tasmania. The morning summer sun made Lawson look angelic. He wore long pants again, good for getting through long grasses and bushes, and hiking boots, a polo shirt that matched the blue of his eyes, but the lack of bow tie was disappointing. We walked toward his Defender, and I pretended that I hadn't checked him out already, focusing on the day ahead instead. "So, what's the plan of attack this morning?" I asked.

Lawson sipped his coffee. "I'd like to investigate the areas where you have seen the Sweet Bursaria plant. The ones we marked on the maps last night. I have three locations marked as a priority, given the northerly aspect. So I thought we could start there."

I had a bag with me today for my laptop and camera, a shovel and soil sample bags, and some data collating. As much as spending time with Lawson was more pleasure than business, I did actually have some work to do.

I put the Esky into the Defender, hooked up Rosemary's harness to the backseat, and climbed in. "Is she all clicked in?" Lawson asked, scanning the rear-vision mirror.

"Yep."

"Does she prefer the window up or down?"

Lawson asked the question so seriously, but all I could do was smile. He treated my dog like her well-being was important to him, and it made my chest all warm and tight. "Down, of course."

Lawson found the right button on the driver's side door and pressed it, and within no time, we were following GPS directions to his first destination. I could have told him where to go, but I liked that he used initiative and didn't rely on anyone else.

As the rain-deprived highway scenery flew by and Rosemary had her nose out the window, I couldn't help but look at Lawson and smile. "Sleep well?" I asked him.

"Yes, very. And you?"

"Very."

"I think your colleagues at the office suspect there might be other reasons you're accompanying me."

"I think you might be right."

He shot me a concerned glance. "Is that... Is that problematic?"

"Nope."

"How do they know? Have you told them of me... and what we're doing?" His cheeks reddened deliciously.

"No. But you called Rosemary by name, and the only place you could have met her already was at my house."

He frowned. "Oh. Of course. I'm sorry. I hope that hasn't put you in a difficult position."

"Not at all. I am actually doing work today, and they won't even know if I happen to sneak in a little make-out session with the sexy lepidopterist during my lunch break."

He blushed properly this time, heat stains running from his cheeks down his neck in the most wonderful way. He dismissed my compliment with an eye roll. "If I ever find an attractive lepidopterist, I'll be sure to pass on your number."

I laughed. "Believe me, I've found one."

"You're absurd."

"If you need me to do a full case-study on this new, exciting specimen of sexy lepidopterist, I'll be only too happy to oblige."

He squirmed in his seat. "And that would involve what, exactly?"

I was grinning, glad he was playing along. "I think the sexual habits need a full review. I'm enjoying the courting rituals so far. I've seen *some* sexual activity, but I don't think I've even scratched the surface yet. But I'm certain this particular specimen is like nothing I've ever known."

Lawson's eyes went from the road to me, then back to the road. He licked his lips and the colour on his cheeks deepened. He shifted in his seat again and cleared his throat. "Is that right?"

God, at this rate we'd be naked before morning teatime. Needing to pull back the tension a bit, I sighed. "Yep. I'm considering giving David Attenborough a call."

Now he chuckled. "I met him once."

"David Attenborough? Get out!"

"But we're not there yet."

I barked out a laugh. "Did you really?"

"Yes, I did. At a gala in Melbourne. He was most charming."

And so we talked about things he'd done, the people he'd met, and the places he'd been until we arrived at our first destination. I really had no idea someone who studied butterflies could live such an interesting life. It was pretty evident that when he didn't have his head in a book, he was out getting things done. Travelling, taking courses, hiking in far off places, all in search of elusive butterflies.

I had to admit, I admired him. Okay, I more than admired him. I was enamoured with, charmed by, and attracted to him.

I couldn't deny it. If there was a list of things that needed to be included in my perfect guy, Lawson Gale ticked every single one. Hell, he even ticked boxes I didn't know needed ticking.

"You getting out?" Lawson asked, his voice startling me from my thoughts. He didn't wait for an answer. He just opened his door and got out. He had the back door open and was getting his gear out a second later. I unclipped Rosemary, and she climbed out and was soon sniffing her way around the clearing.

"Don't go too far," I told her.

"Do you always talk to her?" Lawson asked, putting two stacked plastic storage tubs into the centre of the clearing.

"Of course I do."

Rosemary chose that particular time to inspect what Lawson was doing. Then he spoke to her, "He talks to you all the time, doesn't he?" She wagged her tail and smiled at him in response, and he tousled the fur on her forehead. "I bet you have him wrapped around your little finger," he went on to say to her. "If you had a finger, that is."

"Are you done?" I asked, when the truth was, I could watch him talk to her all day long. I walked over to them with the laptop satchel. "I'm not wrapped around her little finger. I would say I don't spoil her, but I'd be lying. She's my best mate. Of course, I spoil her."

Lawson looked at me then, an amused smirk on his face. "If you didn't, I wouldn't be here. Well actually, that's not correct. *I'd* be here, but you wouldn't be with me."

I scoffed. "Is that right?"

"Yes. What makes you think yours was the only test upon my meeting her?" He raised a daring eyebrow at me. "If I'd have gone to your house and met your dog and it was apparent she was maltreated, I'd have walked away, right there and then, without another word."

Well, I'll be. "So I passed your test?"

He fought a smile now. "With flying colours."

I grinned, then walked over to stand right in front of him. "We might both be technically at work right now, but would you be opposed to me kissing you?"

Something flashed in his eyes like humour, or a challenge. Possibly both. "I'm not opposed. Actually, I rather like it that you asked permission."

I leaned down until my lips barely touched his. "I rather like that you like it." I kissed him then, with open lips and I tilted my head enough to make it playful and perfect. I pulled away, and his eyes slowly opened to reveal a dazed look.

"I rather like it a whole lot more when you don't stop kissing me," he said.

I chuckled. "If I keep going, then I'll keep going, if you know what I mean."

"Oh."

"And I need to keep some secrets hidden for Date Number Three. I'm going for a hat-trick."

He licked his bottom lip and took a small step back, clearly needing some distance. "I'm sure it'll be perfect. No matter what you decide."

The truth was, I hadn't decided what I was doing for dinner. I had no clue yet. "So, work. We better get started or dinner tonight will be eggs on toast."

He opened the first tub and took out his maps. "I like eggs, just so you know. I can eat the finest dining at black-tie galas, but I'm equally happy with eggs on toast. It's the company that matters."

I was grateful he was distracted by his maps so he couldn't see the goofy smile I'm sure I was aiming at him.

"Right, then." I heaved my satchel up on my shoulder. "Work. What are you doing first?"

"Well," he answered, holding the unfolded map out and changing his stance to face north. "I'm going to do a very basic grid formation. I won't be heading any further than two hundred metres in any direction." He then concentrated on his iPad, showing the same map as the paper one at his feet, the same maps we'd dissected last night. He wrote something on the screen, then started to take readings of temperature and barometric pressures or whatever it was he was doing. He was so engrossed in his work, I thought it best to leave him to it.

"Right, then, we'll just be here. Rosemary," I called to my dog. She was sniffing at something thirty-odd metres away, but she was quick to come back when I called her. I told her to lie down under the shade of the Defender, and soon enough she was happily snoozing.

I took photographs of the track we'd driven on, good for condition reports and records. I took soil samples, checking for moisture content. I'd have preferred an auger, but doing it by hand was cathartic. I loved being outdoors, getting my hands dirty, and doing hard, physical work was rewarding. It was hot, and I had worked up a sweat by the time Lawson came back.

"Looks hard," he said, nodding to the hole I was working on. "The ground, I mean."

"It is. We need rain badly."

"Yes, I'm still surprised Tasmania is this dry." He wiped his forehead with the back of his hand. "I understand the entire state isn't prone to high rainfall, but even farmlands in this area which would be typically lush have browned off. Underfoot is very dry."

I nodded. "Department of Meteorology says we should get rain next week. Not that it'll be drought-breaking, but we'll take anything we can get." I noticed then he was still holding his iPad. "How'd you go? Find anything promising?"

He shook his head. "Not yet. I've covered the northeast areas of what we marked out last night. I'll start on the south and west now."

"Need me to help you?"

He gave me a small, thankful smile. "It's fine. It won't take me long, and I'd hate to take you from your hole digging."

I snorted at that. "Soil testing for moisture content, thank you very much."

His smirk in response told me he was only joking. "I'd like to assess a second area after I'm done here. Is that okay with you, or do you need more time here?"

"I'm right to go whenever," I said. "I also packed us a lunch, so just give a holler when you're hungry."

"Oh." He seemed taken aback. "Thank you. That was most thoughtful."

"I try."

"Lunch *and* dinner," he mused. "I'll have to think of ways to repay you."

I raised an eyebrow at him. "While I can think of a few things," I hinted, "I don't actually expect anything in return." I gave our surroundings a quick glance. "This isn't exactly a horrible way to spend my day."

He smiled, and his eyes never left mine. His gaze was intense and somehow playful. "I preferred my suggestion of repayment, but if digging holes does it for you, then I'll keep my suggestions to myself." He turned and walked away, heading toward the line of trees to the south of us.

"I like suggestions!" I called out after him. "You can repay me however you see fit!"

He turned to give me a smile but kept walking. I sighed, resting on my shovel. Damn. He was just getting more and more perfect.

And it was getting more and more hot. Another half an hour of digging baked earth had me a sweating mess, so I took off my shirt. I wiped my face down with it and tucked it into the back of my pants. I was finished digging and was lying down on my stomach, scooping out a sample of soil at 400mm for collection, when someone cleared their throat.

I looked up to find Lawson standing, watching me. And from what I could tell, he liked what he saw. "I got hot," I explained.

He swallowed hard. "I would argue the fact you were hot before the temperature rose. But I won't lie, you shirtless and lying down in the dirt does improve the aesthetics."

I laughed, and putting my hands on the ground near my shoulders, I jumped to my feet. "Is that so?"

He was staring at my chest and stomach, both covered in sweat and dirt. "Mmm."

I might have flexed a little, just for show, as I took my shirt and wiped myself down again. He didn't even try to hide the fact he was gawking at me. When he finally looked at my face, I was grinning. "So? Did you discover any non-existent butterflies in the southwest section?"

His eyes flashed with something like indignation and he tilted his head. I don't think he liked my question. "No."

"Did I say something wrong?"

"Do you think I'm foolish for taking Professor Tillman at his word and spending my time searching the woodlands of Tasmania for a species that might not even exist?"

"What? No, I don't think that at all."

"Would you mind putting your shirt back on please?" He licked his lips again. "I can't seem to concentrate."

"Sorry," I said, not really sorry at all. Seeing Lawson all flustered did great things for my ego. I pulled my shirt over my head.

"I'm not doing this for the glory of it," he added. "Searching for this species."

"I know that." I looked him right in the eye so he would see my sincerity. "No. I think you're passionate, and you love what you do so much that you *want* to believe Professor Tillman. Because what if he's right? Because what if there *is* a species of butterfly never documented before!

And what if you're the one to find it? You're not in this for the glory, even I can see that. You're doing it because if this species does exist, there needs to be research and breeding programs and funding. Finding it is just the beginning."

He didn't speak for a moment, just looked at me like a cryptic riddle in his head finally made sense. "Well, yes." He looked to his feet, then back to me. "No one's ever understood that part of me. Not outside of my work, anyway."

A warmth expanded in my chest at his words. "Then no one's ever paid close enough attention."

"No," he answered quietly. "I guess they haven't."

Changing the subject, I dusted off my hands. "Want some lunch? I'm starving."

We ate our lunch of pastries, bread, and fruits while Rosemary chomped through her doggie cookies, and Lawson started asking me questions about what I did every day. "What do you love about your job?"

"Being outdoors. Days like this: sitting in the shade out in the middle of nowhere. Nothing but peace and quiet and the sounds of birds, crickets."

"What's your least favourite thing?"

"Paperwork."

"Really?"

"I hate it."

"I find paperwork relaxing."

"Relaxing?"

"Yes, it's methodical and predictable. It calms my mind."

"It turns my mind to sludge."

Lawson let out a long breath and smiled serenely. "Well, if this is your office, your view isn't half bad."

"Tell me about your office."

"It's small. Half the size of that of my boss's. I assume it reflects my pay and importance, by comparison also." He smiled, I assumed to let me know he was either joking or he found the humour in the truth of it. "The laboratory is my favourite workspace. Well, not even workspace. Any space, really. But this here…" He looked around. "This isn't too bad at all."

I got to my feet and extended my hand to him. "Come on. Lunch is over."

Lawson allowed me to pull him to his feet, but as I suggested we head to the next area we'd marked on the map, he frowned. "Forgive me if I'm wrong, but I was under the impression that along with lunch there was also making out?"

I laughed at how unashamed he was. "Oh, were you?"

He lifted his chin and fought a smile. His defiance and humour were cute as hell. "Yes. If I recall correctly, you said no one will know if you happen to sneak in a little make-out session during your lunch break."

Now I laughed more genuinely. "Ah, that's where you're wrong." I put my hand to his jaw and lifted his face a little. "I'm pretty sure I said 'a make-out session with the sexy lepidopterist.'"

He rolled his eyes and I crushed my mouth to his. He was startled by the contact, but I held his face right where I wanted him. He melted against me, sighing into the kiss. I tilted my head just enough to deepen the kiss, and he slid his hands around my back.

God, he tasted so good. He fit against me perfectly, and his arms around me felt divine. His hands clawing at my back felt even better…

Rosemary huffed at our feet, making us break apart. She sat there smiling up at us.

I took a step back and let out a laugh, running my hand through my hair. I was a little embarrassed at how carried away I'd gotten. "I uh, I'm sorry. That got out of hand."

"Don't apologise." Lawson thumbed his bottom lip, and Jesus help me, I almost groaned. He had no idea—absolutely no clue—how sexy he was. "I think Rosemary knew she'd better interrupt." He licked his lip and cleared his throat. "Or it could have gotten very out of hand."

I took a very large, very deliberate step back. "Agreed." I turned and pointed to the Defender. "We really should get more work done." I was grasping at my self-control, and if he hesitated in the slightest, even the smallest bit, I doubted I'd be able to stop myself. My dick was half-hard and at an odd angle, and I really needed to adjust…

His line of sight followed my hand, and he swallowed hard. "Work, yes." Thankfully, he turned and started to collect our lunch leftovers, putting them back into the Esky. He gave Rosemary a pat and shot me a hesitant look, his eyes dark. "I think work is a very good idea."

So we did work, all afternoon. We found the next area I'd shown him on his map last night. It was about a kilometre further up on the track we'd taken into the National Park. He did his grid-walk of the area we'd highlighted, and I took more soil samples, took photos of the vegetation, and of a tawny frogmouth's nest. We didn't track every kind of native animal or bird, but noting locations and activity when I could never hurt.

Lawson found nothing again, and even though he said he expected nothing less, I could tell he was a little disappointed. It was in his eyes, and as he drove us back toward town, it was in the way he fidgeted in his seat and the tic in his jaw.

"Tomorrow's another day, huh?"

He brightened some. "Yes."

Just then, my phone buzzed. It was a message from Remmy. *Call past home. I have something for your dinner date tonight.*

I smiled. "You know, I'm pretty sure Remmy thinks I'm useless." I held up my phone to show him the message.

"You told her about our date tonight?"

"Yes, of course. I called in to see her this morning to collect our lunch, remember?"

He nodded. "Oh, right."

"Well, I didn't actually have to tell her anything. She guessed as soon as I walked in."

He glanced at me, then back to the road. "What do you mean?"

I pointed to my face. "The smile. Gave me away, apparently."

His answering smile was slow spreading. "Oh."

"So she's taken it upon herself to prepare something for our dinner tonight. I told her I had no clue what I was gonna cook, but it had to be special, ya know, because of the perfect date pressure you put me under."

He snorted. "I told you I don't need anything extravagant. It's the company and conversation I scrutinise. Not the food."

"Good to know the pressure is on my personality and not anything else."

Lawson laughed. "Exactly."

* * *

After parting ways with Lawson, I knocked on Remmy's front screen door. The wooden door was open to let the breeze in, so I could see inside. I heard little footsteps before I saw the culprit. Luca, all long blond curls and cute dimples, wearing only a pair of shorts, sprang to life in front of the door with a giggle. "UncaJack!"

"Hey tiger," I replied.

Luca roared at me just as Remmy came to the door, wiping her hands on a tea towel. She let me in and Luca launched himself at me. I picked him up. "Jeez kid, you're getting too big! Have you been playing in your mum's garden? You're growing like a tomato plant!"

Luca laughed. "I show you," he said, squirming to get down. I followed him into the kitchen, where he leaned up on his tiptoes so he could reach and pull over a bowl of home-grown vegetables. "These are from my garden." He reached in and took a tomato in one hand, a zucchini in the other. His little fingers barely held them. "I can make ratooey."

"Ratatouille," Remmy gently corrected.

Jeez. The kid was four and was a better cook than me. I guess that's what happened when your parents, French and Portuguese, were chefs. "Make sure you save a seat for me when you do, 'kay?"

The kid beamed before running to the fridge to get himself a drink. He put the jug of juice on the counter, and Remmy watched on as he poured himself a cup. "He'll hold you to that," she said fondly.

"Good. I'll look forward to it."

"Next week?"

"It's a date."

She smirked. "Speaking of dates…" Remmy went to the fridge and pulled out a tray that had some kind of baking paper pouch on it. "For a perfect date tonight."

"You didn't have to do this," I said kindly.

"It was no problem. I was making it for our dinner, so it was easy to make enough for you." She unwrapped the corner of the paper pouch. "I put that twenty you put in my till this morning to good use. It's rainbow trout with a splash of Thai spices. I wasn't sure if Lawson liked spicy food, so I kept it fairly tame. All you need to do is pop it in a hot oven for twenty minutes. It'll steam in the paper. Then serve with steamed veggies and you're golden."

"You're an angel."

Nico walked into the kitchen. "Ah, the man with the perfect date," he said with a warm handshake. "Good to see you, my friend."

I chuckled. "Well, I'm aiming for three outta three in the perfect date score. I think Remmy's almost got me home with this." I gestured to the trout she'd prepared.

Nico rubbed his belly. "Don't know how I'm not the size of a barn." He kissed Remmy's cheek. "The hardships of marrying a pastry chef."

"Well, I don't know what I'll cook for Date Number Four," I said. "Don't know what will beat fresh trout prepared by a chef."

"I cook for you, UncaJack," Luca said. He was kneeling on a stool at the bench next to me, sipping his cup of juice. "I make ratooey."

"Oh Luca," Remmy said. "UncaJack doesn't want us there on a date, darling."

"I don't mind," I said. "And I'm sure Lawson wouldn't either." Because if he didn't want to spend any time with my dearest friends, then maybe there was no long-term hope for us. "We can have dinner at my place. Only if it's alright with you."

"Can I, Mama? Can I?" Luca pleaded.

Seriously, the kid was so stinking cute with those big eyes and dimples.

I gave Remmy my best grin. "Come on, it'll be fun. And I know you're itching to give Lawson the third degree."

Nico snorted out a laugh. "She is."

"Then let me make dessert," Remmy said.

"You're doing enough!" I tried to reason. I knew Luca cooking meant that Remmy was supervising, and by supervising, I meant doing most of it.

Remmy waved her hand in the air, dismissing my concern. "Ah, it's nothing."

Nico gave me a sympathetic smile. "You know she's not happy unless she's feeding someone."

That was true. "Well, thank you. I'm very grateful."

"Wait until after dinner before you thank us," Remmy said, winking toward Luca. "And I suggest you tell Lawson before you drop him into this."

"Ah, where's the fun in that?" I asked. "Let's see how he likes surprises."

Remmy laughed. "I guess it's one way to see someone's true colours." She handed me the tray of trout. "Here. Don't want to keep him waiting. We'll be at your place at six tomorrow night, that way we can be out of your hair by seven thirty." She waggled her eyebrows at me. Nico laughed, and Luca was busy already lining up his tomatoes and zucchinis along the counter.

I gave Remmy a kiss on the cheek. "Thank you. And I'll see you then."

* * *

By the time I got home, I barely had enough time to shower and get some veggies sorted for steaming before Lawson arrived. I heard his Defender pull up and met him at the front door. He'd showered too, and was now wearing brown pants, a faded denim long-sleeve shirt, and his trademark bow tie. He took my breath away. I leaned in and kissed him softly, square on the lips. "Hello there."

He produced a small bottle and frowned. "I wasn't sure if I should bring a gift or token of thanks. I know it's customary for the guest to do so, but I couldn't think of anything that seemed appropriate or that the local supermarket would sell. But I found this, and given it's a local product, and you like to cook, I thought…"

I took the bottle and read the label. It was a locally produced gourmet strawberry coulis. "You don't have to bring anything, but thank you."

He rewarded me with a smile that made my stomach flip. "Something smells amazing."

"Dinner, which I can't take credit for. It was all Remmy's doing. Hope you like a Thai-inspired trout?"

He hummed. "Sounds lovely." We walked inside where he gave Rosemary a welcoming pat, and I thought now was a good time as any to bring up dinner plans for tomorrow night. "Now, I don't want to assume there will be a Date Number Four, but I might have already organised something…"

"Oh?" He leaned against the kitchen counter, completely at ease. "You're that confident to presume a fourth date?"

I shrugged at him. "Confident. Hopeful. Same thing, really."

He smiled and a faint blush covered his cheeks. "I'll have to check my schedule, but I think I'm free."

I chuckled. "Good. Because I have a personal chef lined up to cook here, just for us."

He stared at me. "Are you serious?"

I nodded. "Yep. He's a cutie too. There's a downside, though."

"What's that?"

"We won't be dining alone."

"Oh."

"They've promised to leave early, though. I hope you don't mind."

His blush deepened. "Not at all."

I traced the heat across his cheek with my thumb, then gave him butterfly kisses along his cheekbone. His breath caught, and he slid his hand around my neck and pulled me in for a kiss. Fuck. I pushed him against the kitchen counter, and he deepened the kiss with a groan from the back of his throat.

God, I could kiss him forever.

And just when I took a breath and kissed him again, the microwave beeped and startled us. I laughed at myself for jumping, and Lawson licked his bottom lip. "That would be the rice," I said lamely. I couldn't seem to take my eyes off his mouth. "Which we could totally ignore for a while." I kissed him again, only this time to be interrupted by the oven timer.

He chuckled. "I think the universe is trying to tell us something."

"Yeah. If I burn Remmy's trout, she'll kill me." So I served dinner, which was outstanding. Lawson made a point of complimenting the rice and steamed beans and baby squash, knowing it was the only thing I'd done. But we sipped wine and made small talk about new government environmental protection laws, climate change, and music, but there was an underlying static, a charge of sexual tension that never went away.

It was in every forkful of food, every lick of his lips, and in every sip of his wine. It was in his eyes when he looked at me, in how his fingers held his wine glass. Even the line of his jaw, his neck, the timbre of his voice. Every single thing he did turned me on.

He took a sip of wine and slowly put the glass on the table. "If you keep looking at me like that, I won't say no to whatever it is you want to do to me."

*Oh, fuck.*

I couldn't speak for a second. I had to take a breath first. "I can't help it. And I can't even bring myself to apologise. You're sexy as hell, Lawson, and you have no idea what it is I want to do to you."

His cheeks flamed but his eyes darkened. He held my gaze, daringly. "Does it, in any part, involve your mouth on my body?"

All pretences were down and I was done for. Every nerve in my body was a live wire, and my cock throbbed and my balls ached with need. I stood up, my chair scraping on the floorboards. I walked around to his side of the table, and he never even attempted to stand up. He simply sat there and stared up at me with a knowing, brazen smirk and waited for me to make my move.

# CHAPTER TEN

### *Lawson*

Jack held out his hand, which I took and stood up, but instead of leading me to the sofa or to his bedroom, as I'd hoped he would, he pushed me against the dining table. With my arse pressed into the wood, he pushed his body against mine and kissed me like he owned me.

He pinned me where I was with his body and his arms wrapped tight around me. I could feel his desperation in the strength of his hold. It was possessive and pure desire. He swept his tongue into my mouth, owning every part of me he touched.

He was clearly aroused, his erection pressed hard against mine. He ground against me for the friction we both craved, never breaking his mouth from mine.

A passion had sparked between us that I'd never known could exist. I wanted him with every cell in my body.

He was pressing me so hard against the table, it moved under our weight. I lifted my feet and wrapped my legs around the backs of his thighs, just about to beg him to take me to bed.

He gripped his huge hand around my thigh and just when I thought he was going to hitch my leg higher, even pick me up and carry me to bed, he lowered my foot to the floor. I pulled my mouth from his to protest. I was so turned on, my erection wouldn't recede on its own. I needed him to touch me… "Jack, please."

His lips were plump and wet, his eyes unfocused and filled with a fire I'd not seen before. His chest heaved and his nostrils flared, then slowly, he went to his knees in front of me.

"Oh, God."

He undid my belt, roughly pulling it through the buckle. Then he popped the button and undid the fly like he was about to defuse a bomb. He was taking his time, possibly savouring the moment, and all I wanted was his mouth.

I ran my hand through his hair. "Jack." My tone might have been sharper than I intended.

He looked up at me and smiled. "Yes?"

"Please." I wasn't even ashamed to beg. I was desperate for his touch, his mouth, anything. He pulled the front of my briefs down, finally freeing my erection. But he gave me no relief. I fisted his hair this time. "Just fucking suck me."

He hummed and took the head of my cock into his mouth, finally. The warm, wet heat was exquisite. He sucked me down, tonguing my shaft before pulling off. "I do like it when you curse." He held my cock up and nuzzled the underside. "I can't wait to hear your filthy mouth when I'm finally inside you."

My cock jerked in his hold, and he chuckled again. "That's what I thought." Then he took me into his mouth again, pumping my base with one hand and sucking me hard.

"Oh God. Jack, you're gonna make me come."

He hummed around me, encouraging me to come. With my hand still gripping his hair, I thrust into his throat and he took me. I tried to warn him, but my orgasm shattered through me and I released into his throat.

The room spun as the perfect moment of bliss and ecstasy consumed me. As the euphoric haze dissipated, I saw Jack was now on his feet, smugly licking his lips. He wasted no time in kissing me, sharing the taste of me. I could barely catch my breath and loved every moment.

I pulled him harder against me, and the press of his still-hard cock at my hip reminded me of his need. I broke the kiss. "Your turn."

"You don't have to," he whispered.

I raised an eyebrow at him. "I want it. Please tell me I can."

He let out a low growl that sounded like desperation. "God yes."

I took his hand and led him to his couch. I pushed him back on it and quickly knelt between his legs. I undid his belt, then the button and fly of his pants. His eyes were dark and his chest rose and fell with rapid breaths. He put his hand to my face like he was lost for words. Not breaking eye contact, I freed his cock. The smell of musk and desire made my mouth water.

I looked down then to see his cock. He was well in proportion, big all over. A good eight inches, solid girth, and veins. "Oh, that's beautiful," I murmured. I licked my lips and leaned down, tasting his precome. Salty and sweet and everything I wanted. I licked his head, tonguing his frenulum, eliciting a strangled groan from him. So I took him into my mouth and sucked him mercilessly.

"Ugh." Jack's hips came off the couch. "Fuck, Lawson. Yeah, just like that." He put his hand on my head, and I hummed to let him know I liked it. "So good."

I swirled my tongue along the underside of his shaft and he grunted, so vocal. Every reaction was my reward. I skimmed my hands along his hips, then up and under his shirt, searching out his nipples. I circled each soft nub before gently pinching.

"Oh fuck!" Jack cried. He took rapid breaths and his cock surged in my mouth, so I did it again and again until he flexed underneath me. "Gonna come."

I sucked harder, and he swelled and spurted into my mouth. I swallowed every drop, humming gratefully as I did.

I let him slip from my mouth, and he was the picture of satiation. His arms now hung limply at his sides, his face serene, and his gorgeous cock, glistening under the light, lay across to his hip. He chuckled lazily. "Wow."

I sat back on my haunches, proud that I'd rendered him undone.

He lifted his hand and beckoned me closer with his finger. So I put my hands on his knees and leaned in to kiss him, but he wrapped his arms around me and pulled me onto the couch with him. He lay us both down, somehow, like I weighed nothing, and he sighed contentedly. Then he kissed me, soft and lingering, before he pulled me in for a sleepy hug. Okay, so Jack was the cuddling kind. I smiled against his neck.

"Stay the night," he murmured.

I repressed a sigh. I didn't want to ruin this peaceful mood. But I also wouldn't lie. "I can't."

Jack took a deep, disappointed breath. "When will you say yes?"

"When it's right."

I felt his confusion in his embrace. "Is this not right?"

"This is very right."

"I'm confused."

I chuckled. "I can't stay tonight."

He pulled back, and the look on his face was indeed confused and, if I were being honest, hurt. "It's okay if you don't want to."

I put my hand to his cheek and kissed him. "I have another early start tomorrow."

"Oh, that reminds me. I have a meeting tomorrow. I can't come with you."

I pouted. "That's a shame. I enjoyed having you around today."

He brightened a little. "But don't forget dinner tomorrow. You'll need to be here early, if that's okay? I think the chef extraordinaire is getting here around six, so you might want to get here around six thirty."

"Should I bring anything?"

He shook his head and smiled. "No. But can I make one request?"

"Of course."

"Wear a bow tie."

"Is it a formal dinner?"

"No! Not at all. Very informal, in fact." He bit his bottom lip and adjusted my bow tie, which, with us lying down, wasn't easy. "I just find them really hot."

I chuckled at him. "Then I shall wear my finest."

He gave me his most genuine, eye-crinkling smile. But he never said anything. He just stared into my eyes and I couldn't look away. The intensity of his gaze, the fire burning behind them, made my heart gallop.

"I should go," I whispered, though my tone held no conviction. If he'd asked me to stay right then, I would have said yes. And I was sure he knew it too. He held the power to make me stay or leave, but he knew my wishes, so instead of getting what he wanted, he didn't push.

"Okay." He kissed me softly again. "Text me when you get back to your room. Or in the morning. Or both."

Reluctantly, with a willpower I didn't feel, I got up and fixed my clothes. I gave Rosemary a pat goodbye, and Jack stood on the porch to see me off.

"Oh, wait!" he said, dashing off the porch steps and running into the dark at the corner of his house. He came back a moment later with his hand behind his back and a goofy grin. He stood in front of me and presented me with a sprig of rosemary. "It's not a date without a flower. Though it's not really a flower, but it's symbolic of me and my dog, so it's kind of appropriate."

I took the rosemary, put it to my nose, and inhaled the earthy scent. "It's perfect."

"The date? Or the rosemary?"

I leaned up and kissed his cheek. "Both."

I drove away watching the man and his dog on the front porch, knowing that something had changed. Something irreversible. Something amazing. Something I wasn't sure I would ever get to have given we lived states apart, but out here in the woodlands of north-east Tasmania, I'd found something unexpected, something completely wonderful.

* * *

I found nothing in the woodlands I scoured the next morning. I found chrysalises of *Zizina labradus* and *Pieris rapae* as I had found in the other areas I'd searched when Jack was with me, but nothing on the Eltham Copper.

I ate just an apple for lunch, washed down with two bottles of water, and searched again until four, walking my usual grid, taking notes on observations, checking undersides of fallen bark and large rocks a thousand times. I'd done countless field searches, so I knew patience was key, though it was hard not to be disillusioned. And frustrated. I was running out of days on this trip. Maybe I should ask Jack to re-evaluate the mapped areas.

Mmm… Jack.

My mind kept wandering back to him, making it difficult to focus on my data. Knowing I was running out of days here and running out of days to spend with him exasperated my frustrations.

It was foolish, I told myself. I'd known him for a matter of days, and what we had together was no more than a holiday fling. Not that it was really a holiday; though I technically was on annual leave from my employer, I was still working.

I came to Tasmania in hopes of finding evidence, or proof at least, of a species of butterfly not yet documented. Instead, I'd found myself the kind of man I'd only dared dream of. Of course he had to live in a different state than me; it couldn't be that easy. I had no clue if he wanted to keep in touch when I went back to Melbourne or how we could even make it work. He said his last potential boyfriend didn't want long-distance, but he wasn't opposed to it. But just how did one factor in scheduled weekends, airports, and hired cars into a relationship?

God. Would he even want that with me? Just how far ahead had I let my heart wander unsupervised?

Like I said. It was foolish.

It was a lot of fun and incredible while it lasted, but foolish nonetheless.

I sighed as I loaded my storage tubs back into the Defender. I thought of Professor Tillman and how many decades he'd searched these areas and wondered if I was wasting my time. Had he simply handed the baton over for me to give decades of my life just like he had done? Was this now to become *my* life's work?

I allowed myself to wallow in my disillusionment on the drive back into Scottsdale. It was a pretty little town, and I could see why Jack loved it. Everyone knew him by his first name, said hello in the street. He could walk into any shop in the main street and have a chat with whomever was working. It was a world away from Melbourne. Not just the community feel, either. The cogs turned slower here, and that wasn't a bad thing.

It wasn't a bad thing at all.

Back at my room, I showered and sat on the bed with only a towel wrapped around my waist. I entered my data findings, or lack thereof, into my laptop. When that was done, I seriously considered going back into the bathroom and jerking off to stave off any embarrassing erections that seemed ever-present in the company of one Mr Jack Brighton. Especially if there would be other company attending.

But part of me didn't want to dull the intoxicating hold he had on me. He made my whole body sing, and I wanted him to get the full reward. So, ignoring my own needs, I got dressed for the evening. Jack had said it wasn't formal, but we weren't dining alone and there was a personal chef.

A personal chef? Who on God's earth hires a personal chef? Who even knows one to hire them?

I was excited and nervous for this evening. Each date had been better than the last, and I had no doubt I'd be staying the night soon. Maybe not tonight, but soon enough. I wanted to give myself to him in that way, and I knew in my bones it was only a matter of time. I wasn't joking when I'd said I'd stay when it felt right. Though it felt right every time I'd been there, and the sexual side of me wanted it badly. But my brain said not yet. I would stay the night only after he beds me, and I liked to sample the menu before savouring the main course.

So to speak.

And speaking of main courses, I should pick up a bottle of wine or two to take. I was musing over red or white, given I didn't know what we'd be eating, when I opened my door to leave.

Mrs Nola Bloom stood in front of me with her fist up, as if to knock. "Oh," she said, putting her hand to her heart. I must have given her a scare. But then she looked me up and down. "Oh, how lovely. Going out for dinner?"

"Ah, yes." She tried to look over my shoulder into my room, so I quickly stepped into the hall and closed the door behind me. "Just leaving now. Running a tad late," I added, an excuse not to get stuck talking.

"Where are you off to?" she asked cheerfully. Then she gave me a sly smile. "Dining with anyone I know?"

I cleared my throat. "Ah, no. It's a work dinner. Heading out of town." That wasn't technically a lie. I did see Jack for my work, and he did live out of town. "I best get going, actually. Was there anything I can help you with? You were about to knock?"

"Oh." She blushed, and I knew right then that she was merely here for the gossip on me. "Just checking to see if you needed anything. You've been getting in late every night and leaving early, I wondered if you wanted a decent, home-cooked meal. Or breakfast. It's part of the price you know. No extra charge."

I put my hand up. "No, but thank you. I've been very busy with work, but I'm managing to eat just fine."

"Right, then," she said, stepping out of my way. "Better let you go. Don't want to keep your dinner date waiting."

I repressed a sigh and considered correcting her—she was, after all, only after gossip to feed the town vines, no doubt—but thought it wasn't worth it. "Thank you."

I walked as fast as was polite and got into my Defender. Next stop was the local hotel, which also served as the local bottle shop. I was loath to walk into a small town country pub, but with no other choice, I parked out front and walked inside.

The smell of stale beer assaulted me first, all bar room chatter died away to leave an awkward silence, but the lady behind the counter smiled. "Hey love, what can I get for ya?"

I ignored the eyes I could feel on me from the men at the bar. "Do you have a wine list?"

She handed over a laminated sheet of paper, and not knowing the first thing about wines, I chose the most expensive white, and the most expensive red on the list.

"Sure thing. I'll just grab them from the storeroom. Be right back," the lady said. She darted through a door, leaving me alone with the five men at the bar who were all staring at me.

"Good evening," I said, uncomfortable under their scrutiny.

One man nodded, one man craned his neck to get a better look at me.

"Dressed a bit fancy for round here," one other man said. This is why I hated frequenting establishments like this. I didn't belong and was clearly made fun of by those who felt their masculinity needed protecting. They looked like they'd walked in from Blokey Farmers R Us, and I wondered if they got their flannel plaid shirts at a discounted rate for bulk buying.

The barmaid walked back in with two bottles in hand. "You fellas could learn a thing or two by dressing up a bit," she said with a wink to me. "George, I reckon Bev'd love to get dressed up to go out for dinner with you looking as sharp as this guy."

"Hey," the man I assumed to be George said. "I have a bow tie."

Another man snorted. "From when? Your wedding?"

The barmaid placed the bottles in brown paper bags in front of me. I handed over my card and paid, taking my wine as George was trying to remember the last time he wore suspenders.

I rushed to the Defender and don't think I breathed until I'd turned down Stanning Road. By the time I pulled up in front of Jack's place, I was feeling okay, until I saw another car parked at the side of his house. I'd forgotten he was expecting company other than myself. I took a deep breath, then another. My nerves were getting the better of me, and for a brief moment, I considered going home. But then I remembered he'd hired a personal chef and that I couldn't leave him in the lurch like that. So with another deep breath, I grabbed the wine and made myself get out of the car.

I walked up the porch steps and could hear chatter inside, and the smell of something cooking was wonderful. Rosemary met me at the screen door before I even knocked. She wagged her tail, and I heard Jack say "I'll get it" before he appeared at the door.

Jack's immediate smile when he saw me made me feel a thousand times better. He opened the door with a tea towel in his hand. "Hello," he said quietly, just for me. He leaned in and kissed my cheek. "You look great."

I looked down at myself. "Oh, thank you. I wasn't sure if the suspenders were appropriate, and the fellows at the bar seemed to think I was overdressed."

Jack frowned for a moment. "Did they say something to you?"

"No, it wasn't a problem." I brushed his concern off. I held up my purchases. "I brought wine."

"Please, come in," he said. He slid his arm around my waist. "There's people I want you to meet."

A man was at the dining table, and I wondered if he was the chef. He was average height, had a healthy tan and curly brown hair. "You must be Lawson," he said. There may have been a slight accent, possibly European, but I couldn't be certain. He extended his hand for me to shake.

"Yes, that I am." I shook his hand, and his smile widened.

"I'm Nico. Remmy's husband."

I turned to find her familiar face in the kitchen. Remmy was standing at the counter, and she quickly rounded the benchtop to put her two hands on my shoulders and kissed both cheeks. "Lawson, so nice to see you again. You met my husband, Nico?"

"Yes, thank you."

"And our chef for tonight…" Remmy waved her hand to the small child standing on a dining chair at the kitchen sink. He was peeling a carrot. "Luca, this is Lawson. Lawson, this is my son, Luca."

"Nice to meet you," I said.

Luca grinned. "Hello."

Jack chuckled beside me and put his hand on my back. "Luca, tell Lawson who grew those vegetables you're chopping up?"

"I did!" Luca said. He was a gorgeous little boy with blond wispy curls and a cherub smile. "I did grow them all by myself and UncaJack said I could cook the dinner."

I found myself smiling, grinning even. I couldn't explain how relieved I felt. "That's perfect," I said.

Jack gave me a curious look, so I explained, "I was rather nervous about tonight. I wasn't sure what to expect when you said a personal chef." I almost laughed. "But this is… even better."

Jack went to say something, but Luca spoke first. "UncaJack, your carrot."

"Oh," Jack said, walking to stand next to Luca's chair. He smiled at me. "I'm being the apprentice today."

Remmy laughed. "Lawson, can I get you a drink?"

And so began what was to be a night of laughter and stories, surprisingly delicious 'ratooey,' and even better homemade apple pie. Remmy asked me a slew of questions, Nico was quite well versed in world economics, Luca asked me all about butterflies, and Jack's deep, throaty laughter was quite possibly my most favourite sound.

By the time Luca was falling asleep, Remmy and Nico thanked Jack for a wonderful night, bundled their little one into their car, and bid us both goodnight. The silence after they'd gone was a little loud, but when I turned to look at Jack, he was smiling at me. "You were great tonight."

"How was I great?"

He put his hand to my jaw and thumbed my cheek. "Luca thinks you're the best thing ever."

"He's a great cook. For a four-year-old."

"He is." He ran his hand down my neck and over my shoulder, down my chest. Then he said, "And while I thoroughly enjoyed their company, I missed talking to you. I heard you telling Remmy you didn't find anything in the field today."

"No, nothing."

Jack skimmed his hand back along my suspender, up my chest, and over my collarbone. His smile faded as he licked his bottom lip. "Will you stay for a little bit? You don't have to stay the night if you don't want. But please tell me you'll stay long enough for me to take you out of these suspenders."

"I thought you liked bow ties?"

"I do! Well, I did, but that was before you wore suspenders."

I chuckled at that. "Then I'll be sure to wear them more often."

He leaned in as if to kiss me, but stopped. His eyes flashed with concern. "Earlier tonight, when you bought the wine, you said some guys said something to you? Were you okay? Because on Date Number One, you were dead set against going inside."

"I haven't had the best of luck at such places." He frowned and waited for me to continue. "When I was at university, we were doing a field study in a small town. A few of my classmates thought a trip to the local pub was in order, and I guess a few of the locals thought the way I dressed was comical. Or offensive."

"Oh, Lawson," Jack whispered.

"I had a similar experience at a country pub in New South Wales as well. I believe I can safely assume I am the common denominator in all such examples, so I have avoided putting myself into that situation again."

His frown had deepened. "I'm sorry that happened to you. The guys here aren't like that, but next time I'll come in with you and introduce you, and I'll make sure they know you're with me." He slid both his hands around me protectively. "No one would say or do a thing to you."

I ran my nose along his jaw. "I can take care of myself." I squeezed his arse. "Though I'd prefer if you took care of me."

He hummed and moved his mouth over mine. I pulled back a little. "Jack?"

"Yes?"

"My suspenders are still on."

* * *

I smiled as I pulled up out the front of the Parks and Wildlife office. Jack was standing by a Rural Fire Services truck, talking to a man I'd not seen before, and Rosemary sat happily at their feet.

I'd only left his house eight hours before. Again, I was tempted to stay the night, but I didn't. He took my

94

suspenders off all right. He wanted to take his sweet time with me, but I was so turned on, I begged for his mouth on me.

I swear he drove me crazy just because he could. Because he would rile me up to breaking point until I couldn't bear it another second, and I'd beg and curse at him until he gave me relief.

And I could honestly say, no one had ever taken such thorough care of me. No one had ever treated me like a delicacy. Not like Jack did.

He grinned as he noticed me, waving at me to join him. He was wearing work shorts and a Parks and Wildlife polo shirt, with work boots worn by tradesmen, but oh boy, he'd never looked better. Well, that's not true. He looked better last night when I'd returned the favour of fellatio. He'd looked unbelievable, then, with his head thrown back, his body taut, and muscles flexed as he came… and of course that memory made me blush.

I walked over to where he was still talking to a friend of his. "Good morning," I said.

Jack grinned. "Tony, let me introduce you to Lawson Gale. Lawson, this is Tony Wells. Tony is the local superintendent for the RFS. Lawson's here on official business for the University of Melbourne."

"G'day. Nice to meet you," he said, offering his hand to shake. He was an older man but fit looking. "Jack was just telling me he's heading up into Mount Stronarch today."

"Yes," I replied, hoping I didn't blush any further. "Jack coming with me has been mutually beneficial."

Jack tried not to smile, and I recalled my words.

*Oh dear.*

"I mean, he gets his work done, I get mine done. Separately. On the same trip, that's all."

Tony, thankfully, seemed unaware of my innuendo. He bent and gave Rosemary a pat on the head. "And Rosemary, CEO, overlooks everything."

Jack laughed. "She does."

After a few minutes of small talk, Tony bid us farewell, said it was nice to meet me, and went on his way. Jack watched the RFS truck pull away, then looked at me and laughed. "Jack coming with me has been mutually beneficial?"

I groaned. "I can't believe I said that."

He was still grinning when he collected his things out of his ute. He added them to my Defender. "You ready?"

"I am. Coffee's in the cup holders."

"Perfect," he said. "I'll just go tell Karen I'll be off then."

I opened the rear passenger door to the Defender and told Rosemary to climb up. I harnessed her in, and a moment later was joined by Jack. He slid an Esky onto the backseat next to Rosemary, climbed into the front passenger seat, and buckled himself in. "So?" he asked. "Where are we going to first, in this mutually beneficial arrangement?"

I slipped the Defender into first gear and headed out on the highway. "Do you plan to remind me of that often?"

He picked up his coffee. "Yes. It didn't help that you blushed."

"All I could picture was your face when you orgasmed last night."

Jack choked on his coffee. "Lawson!"

I shrugged. "I'm not at all embarrassed to admit it was highly erotic."

Jack brushed down his shirt, wiping away spilled coffee. "You're picturing it again right now, aren't you?"

I shifted in my seat. "It really was a spectacular sight."

He reached over and took my hand, lifting it so he could kiss my knuckles. "Do me a favour?"

"What's that?"

"Don't ever change."

\* \* \*

After spending the whole morning searching the last areas Jack had marked as known locations of the *Bursaria spinosa* plant in the Mount Stronarch National Park, I'd not found a single trace.

Yes, the plant was there, but there was no trace of *Notoncus* ants. And the Eltham Copper couldn't live without them. There was no evidence of caterpillars, eggs, chrysalises... nothing.

I walked back to the Defender and put my gear in the back but took out the large folded map.

Jack came over. "What's wrong?"

"Something isn't right." I unfolded the map and laid it on the ground. I weighed each corner down with rocks and studied the area. "Either the area is wrong or Professor Tillman was wrong, or if he had seen them here, they're not here anymore."

"He did see them a long time ago," Jack reasoned. "What can change in a species' life cycle over fifty years?"

Well, when he put it like that... "Everything."

Jack's brow furrowed. "Maybe. But the fundamentals can't. Evolution takes longer than a few decades. So tell me, and I'm being serious, what can change? Or what is most likely to change in that time frame. Look at it objectively, Lawson. Break it down into categories and reassess your search."

I stared at him. My first reaction was to tell him not to tell me how to do my job. But he was right, and putting my ego aside, I took his suggestion as a learning tool instead. "Migration patterns. Their diet won't change. They can adapt, yes, but their food source of choice is *Bursaria spinosa* and that *is* available, so it stands to reason they would eat it if they were here. Migration patterns could change, yes. I can't dispute that, but there are no *Notoncus* ants."

Jack considered what I'd said. "Explain the triangle of dependency thing again."

I'd only mentioned that once to him before in the very beginning, and it thrilled me that he'd remembered it. "You have the Eltham Copper butterfly, *Bursaria* plants, and *Notoncus* ants. The butterfly will lay its eggs in the roots of the *Bursaria*. Larvae live within the underground nests of the ants and emerge at night to feed on the *Bursaria* leaves. The ants protect the butterfly larvae while they feed, and in return, the ants feed upon sugar secretions from the larvae. It's a rather complex plant-butterfly-ant-ecological interaction."

Jack tilted his head. "So, maybe it's not the habits of the butterfly that's changed. Maybe it's the ants."

*Of course!* I smiled at him. "You're very insightful."

He grinned. "Thanks."

"So, in your observations of the parklands in your jurisdiction, have you ever noticed ant colonies?"

"Only about two thousand. But I don't know what the *Notoncus* ant looks like."

"Oh, that's easy. The frontal *carinae* are weakly arched or straight along—"

Jack put up his hand to stop me. "Stop. You're speaking to a civilian. Are they black or brown? Big or small? Do they look like a green ant or a meat ant?"

I smiled at him. "Sorry. *Notoncus* ants are the small black or brown common ant found in open soil or under stones and logs on the ground. Found in your garden, parks, everywhere, really."

"Well, that narrows our search down to the entire state."

Now I laughed. "It does."

"Then why are you so happy?"

"Because I was getting frustrated and disheartened, but this gives my search a new focus."

He cupped my face in his huge hands and kissed me. "So tell me, where do you start from now?"

I sighed and enjoyed the moment before I kissed his palm and looked back down to the map on the ground. "I can discount what I've searched so far. There are no traces of the *Notoncus*. Maybe I should study more on their changing migration habits and favoured climes." I stared at Jack while my mind worked over some long-remembered facts.

"What?"

"You mentioned the *Iridomyrmex*."

"No, I didn't. I can't even say that word."

I snorted. "Also known as meat ants."

"Ah, those I did. Bastards bite."

My smile was slow spreading. "They also inhibit the morphological and behavioural adaptions of the *Notoncus*."

Jack blinked. "And that's important because…?"

"I noticed a few nests not far from the areas I've searched."

"And the *Notoncus* won't go near them?"

I shook my head slowly. "No, they won't."

"So, we need to find areas where there are no meat ants?"

I nodded. "Yes."

"How do you find that?"

"The *Notoncus* will live anywhere. Any type of soil, under rocks, bark, anywhere really. But the *Iridomyrmex* is soil-specific. You've been taking soil samples, yes?"

"Yes. As part of our ecosystem analysis. So we can see patterns of average climate changes, soil degeneration, moisture content, pH levels, vegetation quality, all at a glance."

I picked up the map and folded it. "You," I said, leaning up to kiss him quickly, "are a godsend." I opened the rear passenger door of the Defender and called for Rosemary to get in.

As I was harnessing her in, Jack asked, "Where are we going?"

"To your office. How many years' worth of data have you got?"

"Uh, our records go back fifty-something years."

I was grinning when I threw him the keys. "You drive. I need to research a few things on the way."

\* \* \*

"Oh, you're back early," Karen said as we walked into the office.

"Yes, we need to access some archives," Jack said. "They're all electronic now, aren't they?"

"Sure," Karen said, quickly typing something into her keyboard. She turned the screen around, showing banks of data files all sorted by year. "Even photographs have been uploaded."

Jack clapped his hands together. "Excellent. That will save us about a decade." Then he stood back, making a point of looking at me. "Lawson here needs access. We'll be in my office. Could you please bring me the geotechnical reports we have on hand?"

"Sure," Karen said brightly. She gave Rosemary a pat with an odd kissy noise and spoke to her in a baby voice before disappearing down a hall.

Jack led the way into his office. "This way." He sat behind his desk and brought his computer to life. "Hey, Robert?" he called out.

"Yes?" came a voice, I assumed Robert's. A moment later, a short, middle-aged guy appeared in the door. "What's up?"

"Can you remember off the top of your head what type of soil is predominant in the North Scottsdale Forest Reserve?"

Robert thought for a moment. "I think it's basalt, but I'd have to double-check. We ran that core sample last year, remember?"

Jack nodded. "Yeah, that's what got me thinking." Then he looked at me. "What type of soil did you say the meat ants like?"

"Typically clay or clayey soil."

And for the rest of the afternoon, we cross-referenced years of ecosystem data with photographs, soil reports, and rainfall data. Jack and I sat side by side and worked perfectly together. We almost had a conclusion down when there was a soft knock at the door.

Karen stood there smiling fondly at Jack. He cleared his throat and a light blush covered his cheeks. "Yes?" he asked.

"It's five o'clock," she said. "You two staying or calling it a day?"

"We're almost done here," I said.

Jack nodded. "We'll close up. Thank you, Karen." She waved us off, and she and Robert left, and the office was quiet. Jack tidied the piles of paper in front of us. "Wanna call it a day?"

"Yeah. I think we've got enough to know where to start tomorrow."

"Dinner at my place?"

"I don't want to keep relying on you to feed me," I said. "You've gone to a lot of trouble to impress me with dates."

"I promise there will be nothing fancy about dinner tonight."

"But I'll still be impressed? It is Date Number Five, I believe."

Jack laughed warmly. "I think so, yes."

We packed up our work and closed and locked the office. Instead of saying goodbye, I said, "See you at your place in half an hour."

* * *

A quick shower later, I was dressed for a casual dinner, and I was fairly sure how this night would end. I packed a bag of toiletries and supplies and some clean clothes for tomorrow I could leave in the car if needed. I called into the store on my way and bought some locally

Imago                                                    N.R. Walker

mulled honey cider, some local cheeses, apples, and crackers, and at the checkout there was a stand of small posies. They weren't anything fancy, probably lame by most standards, but I picked a yellow collection of daisies, and added them to my purchases.

Fifteen minutes later, I pulled up at the front of Jack's place. Leaving my overnight bag and clothes in the car—in case it didn't work out as planned—I grabbed my bag from the store and made my way up his porch steps.

He must have heard me pull up. "Door's open," he called out.

Rosemary met me with a wagging tail and toothy smile, and I found Jack in the kitchen. He wore old jeans and a faded T-shirt, bare feet, and he looked incredible. He was putting something into a basket.

"I bought these," I said, putting my purchases on his kitchen counter. Then I held out the flowers. "These are for you. You've given me a selection of flowers, so it was only right that I return the gesture."

"Thank you," he said, planting a soft kiss on my lips. He took the flowers with a heart-stopping smile and rummaged through a cupboard until he found what he was looking for. An old jam jar became a vase. He added some water and placed them on his kitchen windowsill. He looked particularly pleased.

I took the items I'd bought from the bag and showed him the cider, and he read the label of the cheese. "So perfect." He grabbed two glasses from a cabinet, a knife from the drawer, picked up the basket, and nodded toward the back door. "This way."

I'd never seen his backyard, so I followed him keenly. His yard was huge; a green field of mowed grass was like a shoreline to a rolling paddock of woodlands. There were shrubs and flowers and a clothesline in the corner with some tea towels swaying in the breeze, but that wasn't what captured my attention.

102

In the middle of his lawn, he'd laid a blanket, some cushions, and pillows. Jack put the basket he was carrying on the blanket and turned to me and waved his hand at the picnic. "Your dining table tonight."

I was certain I was grinning like a crazy man. I put my hand to my heart, feeling the tempo through my shirt. "This actually couldn't be more lovely."

He sat his huge frame down on the blanket and spread his long legs out, leaning back on his elbow. He patted the space beside him. "I believe you fit here."

I joined him on the blanket and took his face roughly in my hands. I planted a hard kiss on his lips. "I believe I do."

He opened the basket and took out a container of small sandwich triangles. "Hungry?"

I chuckled. "I haven't eaten sandwiches cut like this since I was at primary school."

Jack grinned and held one perfect white triangle out to me. "Vegemite? Or peanut butter?"

"Either is fine."

Rosemary came sniffing over and Jack roused on her. "She'll steal the peanut butter ones if you're not careful."

I patted the blanket between us and called her over. "Lie down," I said, and she did. I gave her a scratch under the ear, and Jack was staring at me, smiling.

He bit into his sandwich. "Are you here for me or my dog?"

"Both. And we shouldn't exclude her. I don't want her to think I'm the reason she's not getting one hundred per cent of your attention."

He ruffled the hair on the top of Rosemary's head, then he leaned in and gave me a peanut buttery kiss. He didn't say anything, just smiled serenely as he lay back down. He shoved a cushion under his head and ate another sandwich triangle. "So, how is this date stacking up so far?"

I looked around as evening settled over the countryside. The sun was behind the house, the sky was a palette of blues and oranges, the air was cooling down what had been a warm summer day. "It's kind of perfect."

He sighed happily. "Glad you like it."

Just then a common white butterfly flitted along the breeze near us. "Ooh," Jack said. "What kind of butterfly is that?"

"A *Pieris rapae*. Or a white cabbage butterfly."

"Is there anything you don't know about butterflies?"

I considered his question. "I think there are always things we don't know. But about the recognised species already discovered, I know all there is to know. Though I'd hate to think we've learned all we can."

He smiled up at the sky as though my answer truly pleased him, and he absentmindedly played with Rosemary's fur.

I poured us two glasses of the honey cider, and Jack took one gratefully. Then I sliced the apple and cheese, opened the crackers, and fed him alternate mouthfuls. I liked taking care of him. He had, after all, provided four dates where he'd cooked for me, so it was the least I could do.

When we'd eaten enough of our picnic and the bottle of cider was almost gone, we discussed things such as biodiversity right down to music and movies. The sky was almost darkened through by then, but the backlight of the house cast enough light so we could still see.

Rosemary had wandered off after all the cheese was gone, and I lay down with my head in the crook of Jack's arm. We watched the sky become night, and the cider had given me a pleasant buzz.

Jack seemed content to just lay there, but I wanted more. I had come here with the intention of letting him take me to bed, but he seemed equally content to just lay under the stars with me in his arms. And it *was* perfect, but the urge, the desire in my blood wouldn't let me not try…

I turned in his arms and slid on top of him. I let my legs fall on the outside of his, and I leaned on one arm, my face just an inch or two from his.

His smile was surprised and warm. "Oh. Hello."

"I'm testing a theory."

He put his hand to my face and brushed my hair from my forehead. "And what's that?"

"That I can improve on perfect."

I kissed him softly at first, tilting my head just so, for the best angle. He opened his mouth for me, and I deepened the kiss, a charge of warmth filled me when our tongues touched. I put a hand beside his head so I could grind on him, needing the friction, needing to feel his strength underneath me.

He seemed to understand, or maybe he felt the same because he wrapped his arms around me. I was caged by his powerful hold, his hands were warm on my back, and I felt safe, adored, yet I was the one who set the tempo and rhythm.

I rubbed my erection against his through our clothes. The combination of both heat and hardness was both everything I needed and nowhere near enough. I rocked my hips, grinding on his cock, and he moaned into my mouth.

So I leaned back on my knees. He was a glorious sight. His shirt had ridden up enough to show me the skin above his waistband, his lips were flushed and swollen, he was breathless and beautiful.

I undid the button of his jeans and carefully unzipped the fly. I slid my hand underneath the elastic of his briefs and freed his cock. Sweet Lord have mercy, he was heaven on earth. His skin was silver in the moonlight and a drop of liquid shone at his slit. I leaned down and licked him, moaning at my salty reward.

"Oh, Lawson," he murmured.

I smiled at him and undid my pants, and his nostrils flared and his breath caught. It was intoxicating to be in such control of him. I drew out my cock and gave myself a few strokes while he watched. The look on his face was complete awe and pleading. I shuffled up until our cocks aligned, and when I took him into my hand and slid our cocks together, Jack's eyes rolled closed. He whispered, "Oh fuck."

It was kind of clumsy but he didn't seem to mind. In fact, he writhed with pleasure. His hands found purchase on my shirt, my neck, my face, and he brought me in for a hard, deep kiss. When we needed air, he pulled away. "God, you're gonna make me come."

I stroked our cocks harder, using our mix of precome as lube. "I wanted to have you inside me tonight, but I couldn't wait. I needed to feel you now."

He slid his hand along my jaw, his thumb at the corner of my mouth, and I took it in between my lips and sucked on it.

Jack flexed hard underneath me, and his cock surged in my hand. Pulse after pulse of come spilled from him, and the sight, the smell, tipped me over the edge.

The coil in my belly sprang, and the ache in my balls bloomed into pleasure, and I came on him. Jack held me while my orgasm rolled through me, and he caught me as I collapsed on top of him, utterly spent.

There were no other sounds but our breathing and the hammering of our hearts. Jack kissed the top of my head. "I think you kind of rewrote perfect."

I snorted indelicately, still too boneless to do much else. "I think that orgasm just rewrote my DNA."

Jack roared with laughter, the sound echoed loud and warm through my ear pressed to his chest. "That good, huh?"

The haze started to lift from my brain, and I realised I'd just done all that to him outside. Thank God he had no close neighbours. "Um, I've never had sex outside before."

He chuckled and gave me a squeeze. "Me either. I think there's a little devil inside you that likes to come out to play in the bedroom."

I lifted my head and looked around. "Strange bedroom."

He grinned, but then he turned serious. His eyes were dark and deep. "I will have you in my bedroom one of these days."

I put my fingers to his lips, then replaced them with my lips. "Yes, you will."

Before he could reply, I jumped up to my feet and tucked myself back in. "We should go inside and get cleaned up."

I started to pack up our picnic. He was quick to join me, collecting the blanket before leading the way back inside. "I can get you another shirt," he said.

"It's okay. I brought a change of clothes. And an overnight bag…"

It took him a second to catch on. "Are you staying?"

I nodded, and the grin he gave me was something I'll never forget. It made my stomach flip. "I'll just go grab it."

I took my bag from the Defender and Jack met me at the door. I stepped inside, he lifted my chin, kissing me sweetly, then he closed the door behind me.

# CHAPTER ELEVEN

## *Jack*

After we showered and dressed for bed, I pulled back the covers and hopped in, then extended my arm out in invitation. He was cute as hell in his chequered sleep pants and plain T-shirt, and he bit his lip as he climbed in beside me.

I turned the bedside lamp off and quickly pulled him into my arms. I snuggled in a bit and kissed the side of his head, and he relaxed immediately.

"Just because you're in my bed doesn't mean I'm going to ravish you," I whispered into his hair. "Not saying I won't either, but the DNA-rewriting orgasm you gave me half an hour ago kind of took the edge off."

I could feel him smile against my chest. "This is just as good. Actually, this is very good."

I sighed, and a contentment settled over me like sinking into a warm bath. Sleep was quick to come for us, and the last thing I remembered was thinking that morning sex sounded pretty damn good.

\* \* \* \*

"Wake up, sleepy head."

I frowned and reached in the bed for Lawson, but I found only cold sheets. I cracked one eye open. He wasn't in bed, he was standing beside the bed with a coffee cup in his hand.

"I made this for you."

I groaned as I stretched out. The weight of my morning wood lay heavily across my hip. "What happened to morning sex?"

He laughed and put the cup on my bedside table. "I have butterflies to find."

It was hard to be frustrated or even disappointed when he was so damned cute. He was basically vibrating with excitement.

"I'll make toast," he said on his way back out the door.

I sat up and sipped my coffee with smiling lips. Mmmm, it was good. "I could get used to this," I mumbled.

"What was that?" he called out from the kitchen. There was a clanging of plates and cutlery.

"Nothing," I replied, smiling at the empty doorway. The truth was, I liked having him here. I liked the sound of someone else pottering about, and I really, *really* liked the fact it was Lawson.

After a bathroom stop, I made my way to the kitchen to find Lawson buttering two pieces of toast. He proceeded to spread one with peanut butter and one with Vegemite without asking me which I wanted and slid the plate toward me. He picked up his own coffee and sipped it. "Hope you don't mind. I made myself at home."

"Not at all."

I picked the peanut butter toast, Lawson took the Vegemite piece, and he smiled as he ate it. "So, will you be joining me again today?"

"Would you like me to?"

"Yes."

A thrill ran through me at his direct reply. "Then I shall join you."

Lawson put the plate in the sink as he finished his toast, and he wiped down the countertop. He was babbling because he didn't know if Rosemary usually had breakfast, but he didn't want to give her something she shouldn't have. He was trying to hide his excitement, but he really was buzzing. "Okay, okay," I said, washing my toast down with coffee. "I'll go get dressed."

He breathed a sigh of relief. "Thank you."

I walked up the hall to the bathroom and called out behind me, "And there's some of Rosemary's favourite treats in the container in the laundry."

When I was showered, shaved, and dressed for a day in the field, I found Lawson standing at the back of his Defender. Rosemary was sitting in the back next to the tubs, and he was running through his inventory with her.

"Your office assistant is a cutie," I said.

Lawson chuckled. "She is."

"I was talking to Rosemary."

Lawson's mouth fell open, but I could see it in his eyes when he realised I'd just called him a cutie. "I'm not her assistant."

"Of course not."

"That would assume her in a position of authority over me."

I leaned against the rear of his Defender and grinned at him. "Have a problem with that?"

He never missed a beat. "The only person I want in a position of authority over me is you." He raised an eyebrow. "I have every intention of that happening tonight, but if you don't help me get to North Scottsdale National Park in the next thirty minutes, it won't be happening at all."

I stood up straight and clapped my hands together. "Right. Who's driving?"

* * *

North Scottsdale National Park was northeast of where he'd searched before, and the only access in was a dirt road, as the name suggested, north of Scottsdale. The areas we'd marked out yesterday on Lawson's maps were estimated areas of silted clay on the town side of the mountain. Still classed as dense woodlands, the undergrowth was thicker.

Theoretically, on paper, an Eltham Copper wouldn't inhabit an area like this. But Lawson was adamant. Everything pointed to this location. A combination of the correct soil types, average rainfalls, and temperatures suitable for *Notoncus* ants. From the photographs of the area taken over many years, there was proof of *Bursaria*, but we wouldn't know for sure until we got there.

But more than that, Lawson's gut told him this was where he would find it.

I helped him unpack his tubs and waited for him to get ready. "What will you do if you find a whole... colony of them?"

He didn't even look up. "Colony of what?"

"A colony of the Eltham Coppers that aren't actually anywhere near Eltham."

"A kaleidoscope."

"A what?"

"The collective noun for a group of butterflies is called a kaleidoscope."

"Oh." Then I thought about that. "That's actually pretty cool."

He looked up from his iPad and smiled. "It is."

"Who gets to name the collective nouns? Because they're all very clever. An army of ants, a pounce of cats."

"A flamboyance of flamingos," he added keenly.

"A flamboyance? Who the hell named that? Actually, who the hell *knows* that?"

"I know that."

"Yes, but you're a genius." Then I thought about that too. "Actually, a flamboyance of flamingos is pretty clever."

Lawson smiled. "An array of hedgehogs."

"A cackle of hyenas."

"An ambush of tigers."

"A parliament of owls."

"A congress of gorillas."

"Oooh, that's a good one," I said. "I take it I'm not the only one who finds the collective nouns interesting."

"I used to read them when I was little."

That made me smile. The thought of a little Lawson with his nose in a book, no doubt. "When did you catch your first butterfly?"

"I was four."

"Wow. That's young."

"My grandfather was an enthusiast. He gave me a catching kit for my fourth birthday."

"A catching kit?"

"Yes, you know the green and orange kits with a plastic cylindrical holding jar with a small net."

"Oh, I had one of those. I caught grasshoppers."

Lawson smiled as he scrolled through something on his iPad. "Then the following Christmas, he gave me a proper kit with an actual killing jar. I was very excited."

"About getting a killing jar?"

"It's not the most favourite part, and truthfully it's more humane than the old practices of stabbing an entomological pin through the thorax. And it's only a rarity that any individual butterfly is killed these days. We have such good technology for studying them that we don't need to." He smiled sadly. "I remember when I caught my first monarch, my grandfather made me put it in the killing jar. It was quick, but it was awful to watch. I cried for days."

"Oh, that's horrible." I went to him and put my hand on his arm. "I'm sorry."

He gave me an honest, appreciative smile. "Thank you. But I was five."

"And it drove you to spend your life dedicated to protecting the species?"

He laughed. "It wasn't quite that dramatic, but something like that."

I kissed his cheek. "So, if you do find one of these butterflies, what do you do?"

"Photograph, video, record data." He took a deep breath. "And make some phone calls."

"Is there a Butterfly Justice League or something that sends out a protective detail?" I joked.

He smirked at me. "There is. You're looking at it. Do I detect an inner nerd familiar with Justice League?"

I barked out a laugh. "There is a lot you don't know about me, inner nerd included."

He chuckled again. "I never was one to back down from a challenge." He scrolled and swiped at his iPad screen. "Later though, if you don't mind. Right now, I have much BJL work to do."

"BJL?"

He rolled his eyes. "Butterfly Justice League."

I laughed as I left him to do his thing. I went about my own data collection, taking photos and soil samples. He was quicker in his assessments this time. Still methodical and thorough, but there was a pressure and urgency now. The additional information gave him extra drive, and it compounded his disappointment when he found nothing.

He'd assessed three sites before lunch. He concentrated on the areas of preferred soil type, did his grid thing, and came up empty-handed.

His mood wasn't exactly a happy one as I offered him some lunch. He bit into his apple and frowned as he chewed. "I've found grass blues and common whites, so it's feasible the Eltham might be here."

I knew there wasn't much I could say that would make him feel any better, so I listened to him instead.

"Professor Tillman spent the better part of six decades looking for this particular species. You know what? I don't think I'm cut out for that. I understand patience is key, and I was foolish to think I could find it in a week."

"You've made great progress."

He took another bite of his apple, chewed, and swallowed it down. "Am I supposed to spend every weekend of the next fifty years searching every national park in the state?"

I shrugged. "Yes."

He went to reply but stopped, and his shoulders sagged. Instead he took a deep breath. "I guess so."

"You know it might not be all bad. You'll go back to Victoria but get to come back every weekend you can. I'm not opposed to seeing you on weekends."

Lawson opened his mouth, then promptly closed it. "I don't want to think about that just yet."

"About seeing me again?"

He shook his head slowly. "No. About not seeing you again."

I stepped in front of him and put my hand to his face. "I don't want to think about it either, but we're running out of days, Lawson." I kissed him softly. "When do you leave?"

"In three days."

I sighed, closed my eyes, and pressed my forehead to his.

Three days.

"This is kind of insane, isn't it?" I asked. "I've only known you for a few days."

"Five days. Six days if you include today." His blue eyes met mine, our foreheads still touching. "It's not insane. Insanity is a state of mind which prevents normal perception and/or behaviours."

I chuckled at his clinical reply, but he pulled back so he could see my face properly and shrugged. "Jack, what I perceive of you, and how I've conducted myself in your company is with full mental cohesion." His cheeks stained with colour. "And Einstein would have you believe that insanity is doing the same thing over and over again and expecting different results." He bit his lip and laughed at himself, I think. "But I don't want different results. I wouldn't change a thing."

I kissed him, deeper this time. It wasn't a kiss that was leading to something more. It was simply an I-have-to-kiss-you-right-now kind of kiss. He'd just professed how he felt to me, as only Lawson could. By giving me a clinical definition of insanity and quoting Einstein, of course.

I ended the kiss with a flutter of butterfly kisses against his cheek. "I wouldn't change a thing either," I whispered. "Except for the whole leaving thing."

"Except for that."

* * *

We drove further north, deeper into the national park, the track now no more than a four-wheel drive fire trail. The terrain went from undulating woodlands to steeper, open forest. The canopy wasn't exactly touching but the undergrowth was thicker and made for difficult assessment of possible activity.

But it didn't stop him. I doubted much would. Again, he did his own research and I did mine, though I could hear him whistling or muttering to himself periodically, so I knew where he was at all times.

But he found no *Notoncus* ants, and therefore, no Eltham Copper butterfly.

There was nothing at the second site we went to after that either.

Cloud cover was starting to roll in from the south, which troubled me. After Lawson had thrown his storage tubs into the back of the Defender, he pulled off his hat and wiped his sweaty forehead. "The humidity is rising."

I pointed to the sky. "Those clouds are coming from the south, too."

"And that's not a good thing?"

"Usually means storms."

He sipped his water bottle and moaned. "Please let it rain. It's so dry and hot. Never thought I'd miss Melbourne weather. This here never changes. Back home we'd be onto our third season of the day by this time: arctic southerlies, desert westerlies, monsoon rain. This here is just plain old hot and dry."

I put my hands out and felt the sweat roll down my back. "This is a perfect summer day." Truth be told, it was stinking fucking hot and dry as a chip.

Lawson rolled his eyes. "What's your favourite season?"

"All of them."

"You can't love all of them."

"I do. In summer, I love winter. In winter, I love summer."

Lawson laughed and threw his water bottle at me. I caught it easily and finished it off. "We'd better get heading back. That road in isn't going to be easy going if this storm hits."

He nodded reluctantly.

"I'm driving," I announced as he buckled Rosemary into her seat harness. "There's something I want to show you. It's not far from here."

I followed the trail further north—the overhung branches scraped up the side of the Defender—and pulled off at a closed gate. "Is that private property?" Lawson asked.

"No. It's all Park's land, but we closed access. It's not locked, but it keeps the innocent people out. Plus, most people who use this road are heading through to Bridport. They don't stop along here." I got out and opened the gate, pushing it into the scrub to keep it open. I jumped back in and drove the Defender through and kept on going.

"Shouldn't we have closed the gate?" Lawson asked, looking behind us. "Rule of thumb in the country is, you leave gates as you find them."

I grinned at him. "I know, but we won't be long."

I drove for maybe a hundred metres, but with the winding and bumpy trail, it was slower going than I'd have liked. When I got to as far as the trail would take us, I stopped the Defender and undid my seatbelt. "We walk from here. It's not far, but we'll have to be quick."

Lawson was excited but cautious. "Should I be worried? Maybe my first impression of you being a serial killer was founded."

I laughed as I got out. I opened up the back door, unclipped Rosemary, and pointed directly ahead. "This way."

We'd only been walking for a little while to a symphony of birdlife when he asked, "How far are we going?"

"Almost there. See the clearing up ahead?" As we entered the clearing, I could see the sky had darkened considerably. "Okay, we need to be quick. This way."

I took us to the right of the clearing where a gully formed before the line of trees. I jumped down into the gully and back into the treed area and held onto Rosemary's collar.

"Why did you stop?" Lawson whispered.

"Look over there, twenty metres through the gully." I nodded ahead. "Listen."

He craned his neck and his brow furrowed as he concentrated. I could hear it, and I waited for him to. His eyes flashed to mine. "What the hell is that?"

The noise was very distinct. Growls, hisses, screams, and screeches. It sounded like there were younglings. My grin got wider. "We can look. But we can't get too close."

Lawson's gaze searched and searched, and I could see the moment he found them because he smiled. "Tasmanian devils."

I nodded excitedly. "And joeys. They're very vocal."

We could see two baby devils rumbling and jumping on each other. They were the cutest things. Black with bands of white across the chest, little tails, and huge jaws.

"There's been a den here for years. The same female comes here to have her babies year in, year out. We've been keeping an eye on them. The bitch has been tagged, but she's healthy, her joeys are healthy, so we leave them be."

117

Then a third joey pounced onto his siblings and more growling and snarling ensued, followed by more rumbling and rough-play.

I took out my phone and snapped photographs. "I'll send these to the STDP."

"What's the STDP?" he asked, not taking his eyes off the playful joeys.

"Save the Tasmanian Devil Program," I explained. "We give them any information we can. They do some great work."

"Where's the mother?" Lawson asked.

"She'd be sleeping, probably. With one eye open on this lot, I'd say. They're nocturnal mostly, but will bask in the sun." I watched the joeys play. "Cute, huh?"

"Oh, Jack, they're remarkable."

It was silly how his words could cause my heart to skip a beat. But his love for and understanding of what I did made me happier than I could explain.

He put his hand on my arm as he took a small step and leaned so he could get a better look. Thunder rolled overhead, and I looked up at the sky. "Come on. It's time we weren't here."

We climbed up the embankment of the gully, and I headed left, back toward the way we'd come. I only got a few steps with Rosemary when I realised Lawson wasn't with me. I turned to find him stopped, staring in the other direction.

"Lawson, we gotta get going."

Without looking at me, he put his hand up. "Wait one sec…"

I barely heard him over the rumble of the sky. "Lawson—"

But he was already walking in the wrong direction, over to the far edge of the clearing. He stopped and looked up. "What direction is this?"

"Uh, north, I think. Why?"

He was inspecting something near the trees. "Jack! Jack, come quick!"

I ran over to him. He was now crouching down, lifting the bottom of a shrub off the ground.

A *Bursaria* shrub.

He was looking at ants…

Oh, holy shit.

Then he put his hands down and leaned real low to look up under the leaves of the shrub.

Ants quickly crawled over his hands. "Lawson, the ants…"

"They don't bite," he said absently, not even looking. Then he lifted the bottom branches of the shrub and gently poked a pen into the roots of the plant. And as if right on cue, a little copper coloured butterfly flittered out and landed right near his hand. Then another, then another.

Lawson fell back in shock, scrambling to stay off his arse, and put his hand to his mouth, his eyes wide. He glanced at me. "Jack."

I nodded.

One butterfly took flight again, skipping across the air before landing back in the shrub. Lawson took his phone out and his hands were shaking so badly he could barely scroll to his camera. He took some photos, then had the presence of mind to switch his phone to video mode. He filmed it, this tiny little creature, as it stretched its wings and skittered to a different leaf.

Thunder cracked through the sky just above our heads, scaring the crap out of both of us. Rosemary whined. "Shit that was close. Lawson, we have to go. Now. We can come back tomorrow, first thing. I promise."

He nodded, took a dozen photos of the ground, the shrub, the clearing, then another quick succession of shots of the butterfly, just as the rain began to fall.

"Lawson, now. Or that road will be impassable."

He spun around and got to his feet. The rain had begun to flatten his hair and made his shirt cling to his chest, but his grin was huge. "I found it."

I grabbed his arm and pulled him along with me. "Come on."

Together, along with Rosemary, we ran back to the Defender. I jumped into the driver's side and Lawson jumped into the back with Rosemary. I threw the Defender into reverse, and looking over my shoulder, I reversed the whole way out down the trail to the gate.

Lawson had harnessed Rosemary in, then jumped out to pull the gate shut. When he got into the front passenger's seat, he was still grinning. Actually, he was buzzing. He stomped his feet and did some crazy laughing dance in his seat. Laughing with him, or at him, I shifted the gears into first and started down the trail. "Seatbelt," I said gently, as he obviously hadn't remembered.

He clicked his belt in. "Jack, I found it!"

"Lawson, it was incredible. And it's so small. I wasn't expecting it to be so small."

"I know!" he said, nodding excitedly. He was still bouncing in his seat. "Oh my God, I need to call the professor." He pulled his phone out and did a quick scroll of the photos again. His hands were shaking. The energy he was giving off was incredible. Even Rosemary was standing on the backseat smiling at Lawson. He took a deep breath and tried to calm himself before he dialled the professor. He hit Call, put the phone to his ear, looked at me, and grinned. "Professor Tillman? This is Lawson Gale." I couldn't hear exactly what the professor said, but Lawson then added, "You'll never guess what I found today."

There was a second of silence, then I could hear the professor's muffled voice, and Lawson laughed. His excitement was so contagious, even I was smiling despite the torrential rain and shitty dirt road.

"I'll send you some photos, to the email you gave me. You can confirm, but I'm confident it's it. Looks like the

Eltham Copper but has five small dots on the hindwing with tapered black edges."

He saw all that detail?

Lawson laughed. "Yes! Yes! I know! It's so remarkable. We're just returning to town now. The weather has turned bad, so once I get to my laptop, I'll forward you what I have... Yes, we're heading back up in the morning, weather permitting, of course."

They spoke briefly before disconnecting the call. He looked at Rosemary, then at me, his grin still firmly in place. "I found it."

I laughed. "So you keep saying."

"I can't believe it."

"Can I ask something?"

"Yes, of course."

"What do butterflies do when it rains?"

He laughed. "They hide. Under leaves, bark, logs, large rocks, anything they can find. That's what they were doing when I interrupted them: trying to get out of the coming rain."

As we came down the mountain, the Defender slipped on the dirt road a few times, and I sighed with relief when we reached the tarmac. Lawson seemed oblivious, because he looked at me and smiled. "Can we please go past my place so I can grab my laptop and a change of clothes?"

"You don't want to just stay there?" Then I added, "With me. I mean I'll come to your place with you."

"I'd rather not. Mrs Bloom is nosey, and I love the privacy your place provides." He waggled an eyebrow at me. "I have plans for tonight, remember?"

"Should we get some wine? I think celebrations are in order, don't you?"

His grin hadn't waned one bit. "I think wine and celebrations are definitely in order."

\* \* \*

After Lawson had raced into the B&B, he came back out with a laptop bag and jumped into the Defender, out of breath and rain running down his face. He looked at the clothes sticking out the side of his bag, then smiled at me. "I multitasked."

I laughed and pulled the Defender up in front of the hotel. "Won't be one sec." I braced for the deluge of rain, though it had eased up a little. It was more wind now. I raced for the front doors of the hotel and ordered two bottles of the same wine Lawson had brought home the other night. When I got back into the Defender, he had his phone pressed to his ear and his smile was gone.

"I am advising of my find, not to gloat, but out of professional courtesy. I most certainly will not be sending photographs until Professor Tillman has confirmed what we both suspect is a new species."

*Okay then.* Someone was having their arse handed to them. I had to admit. Lawson was sexy as hell when he was pissed. I hated that some jerk had ruined his mood, though. It was a monumental day by anyone's standards, and some dickhead was trying to bring him down.

"I'm technically on leave until Monday, so you can do whatever it is you see fit... By all means, please do. You can also tell him to expect a full report from me, which I'm certain he'll love. I'll make a point of dedicating an entire subsection to you and how you've just requested to go against protocol... That's fine, Professor Asterly, but after all the years we've worked together can you tell me what I am?"

Lawson tilted his head as he listened. "Yes, well. That too. But more than being a pain in your arse, I am unbiased to the facts, and I won't be manipulated. It's unfortunate that your emotional reaction is to be hurt, but I can't be responsible for how you feel, Professor... No, that won't be necessary. I'll be in contact with him directly. He can let you know when I will return."

I was almost home by the time he got off the phone. Lawson growled in frustration. "That man is an ignoramus."

"Your boss, I take it?"

"Yes. Ugh. I shouldn't have called. I only did so as a gesture of goodwill, and he seems to think himself invited to come down here. No doubt to have his name associated in some way."

I drove into my driveway and turned off the engine. "Lawson, forget about him. Until he gets here, *if* he gets here. Enjoy tonight, get all your data on file, send it to Professor Tillman, then tomorrow we can go back and you can get all the data you need." I just wanted to see him smile again. "Wanna go in and upload the photos? Get a closer look?"

It worked because his lips twitched until he smiled. "Yes, please." He leaned forward and looked up at the low, grey sky. "That looks like it's set in."

"I can check the meteorology site. See if you can get back up there tomorrow." From the look he gave me, I was pretty sure he was going anyway, rain or not. "Come on." I opened the door and got out into the wind and rain. I unharnessed Rosemary while Lawson made a run for the door with his laptop.

Inside, we dried off with towels. It wasn't exactly cold, but the temperature had dropped some with the storm. "You warm enough?" I asked.

He nodded, but it wasn't convincing. "I might get changed, is that okay?"

"Sure. I'll see what I can organise for dinner."

When he came out, he was wearing his chequered sleep pants and a T-shirt. He looked completely comfortable and at home. It took the breath from my lungs.

He looked down at himself. "This okay?"

I nodded stupidly. "More than okay."

He looked into the pantry where I stood with the door open. I picked up a packet of couscous. "Well, I can do a Greek lamb and couscous thing, or—"

"Tomato soup and toasted cheese sandwiches," he said, reaching in and taking a can of tomato soup.

I chuckled. "You're a man after my own heart." I took the can from him and kissed his cheek. "You go start on your photos. I'll fix dinner."

He stood in my kitchen, looking all kinds of adorable. "I *will* cook for you one day."

I barked out a laugh. "Yes. Yes, you will."

* * *

So he busied himself in the lounge room while I got changed into my PJ's too, heated the soup, and made some toasted sandwiches. The wind howled outside, splashes of inconsistent rain hit the roof, thunder and lightning boomed through the sky. But inside was warm and dry and peacefully, blissfully quiet.

When I walked out with his soup and sandwich, I found him sitting on the floor, leaning against the couch, laptop on his legs, and his eyes trained on the screen with Rosemary asleep against his leg.

It stopped me where I stood. My heart squeezed and my mouth went dry.

Such a simple thing, really. A truly domestic sight that sent a pang of longing through to my core. I never realised it was what I wanted. It never occurred to me that I should yearn for something so basic. Sure, I'd had times of loneliness, but I never thought to myself, *gee, I wish I had someone who would sit on my floor in his pyjamas and do his work with my dog curled up at his side…* well, until I saw it. Now I'm pretty sure I wanted nothing else.

Lawson looked up at me expectantly, oblivious to the profound realisation I'd just had.

I held up his plate. "Dinner's ready. Want it down there or at the table?"

He smiled and my breath caught. Man, I was in trouble. "Down here, if that's okay."

We ate in the lounge room, he on the floor, me on the sofa behind him. The soup was a perfect dinner, homely and all comfort as the weather made a fuss outside. Lawson did what he needed to do while I sat and watched him work. I also played with the hair at the nape of his neck, relishing the wake of goosebumps that followed each trail of my finger. When he declared he'd done all he could do, he pounced on me.

He straddled my hips, resting his arse on my legs, and he planted both hands on either side of my face and kissed me.

And holy hell, it was some kind of kiss.

He rocked his hips back and forth seeking friction. "Jack." He breathed the word into my mouth. "Take me to bed."

I was going to pick him up—I could have easily—so he could wrap his legs around me, but he climbed off and stood in front of me. And waited.

I stood up to my full height, so close our chests touched, and I slid one hand around his jaw and crushed my mouth to his. I could feel his erection poking into my thigh, and he slid both hands over my arse and pulled our hips together. He broke the kiss. "Jack. Bed."

He was getting impatient. And I had to admit, I really liked a bossy bottom. It turned me on to be with a man who wasn't afraid to tell me what he wanted.

I took his hand and led him down the hall to my room. I left the lights off, I could see him just fine. I pulled his shirt over his head and kissed down his shoulder. "You want me inside you?"

He moaned quietly. "Yes." He craned his neck as I kissed back up to his jaw. "God, yes."

I slid my fingertips under the elastic of his sleep pants and pushed them over his arse and whispered in his ear, "I want to taste your arse first."

"Oh god," he breathed.

I gripped his erection and gave him a few languid strokes. "Get on the bed, Lawson. Face down."

He did as I instructed, stepping out of his pyjama pants and kneeling on the bed before slowly lying down. Lightning cracked outside, illuminating the room. God, he looked so amazing. I stepped over to the bedside table and threw a condom and the bottle of lube onto the bed beside him. He fisted the duvet in anticipation.

I knelt on the bed and pushed his legs apart, running my hands up the back of his thighs and over his arse. I leaned in and breathed a slow warm breath over his hole.

"Jack, fucking hurry up."

I loved that he only swore during sex. But apparently me taking my time with him was not on his agenda. "I can't wait to hear your filthy mouth," I murmured against the skin at the base of his spine. Thunder boomed outside and the static in the room amped its charge.

"My mouth isn't filthy," he replied on a whisper. There was no conviction in his voice.

I spread his arse cheeks and ran my tongue up his crack, pressing into his hole. He fisted the sheets at his sides and raised his arse for me. "Oh, fuck!"

I smiled victoriously. "You like that?"

"Yes, please more."

Thunder rolled far off and lightning lit up the sky through the window. His arse was perfect, illuminated by the storm outside. Pale and round cheeks and a perfect, tight hole. He wanted more, so I gave him exactly that. I fucked him with my tongue and he grunted with every pass. But it soon wasn't enough.

"More."

I flipped the lid on the lube and poured a decent drop down his crack, and slipped my finger inside him.

"Mmm," he hummed, rocking his hips for me.

"You love it, don't you?"

"God yes. More."

I added a second finger and curled them, searching for his prostate.

"Oh fuck," he growled.

126

There was another curse word. I'm sure he had more in him. So I played with him a bit, stretching him, testing his patience while turning him on. He slipped his hand under his hips, no doubt to grab his cock. "I need more," he said with a tortured groan. "I need your cock inside me."

There was nothing like hearing him beg.

I pulled out my fingers and he responded by raising his hips off the mattress so he could jerk himself. God, he was so hard and so desperate for it.

I rolled a condom down my length and slicked myself up with lube, then added more to his arse. He hummed an impatient sound. "Jack, I need you now."

I knelt behind him and swiped the head of my cock up and down his crack. He rocked back and forth, wanting, needing. "This what you want?"

"Fuck yes."

I did it again, this time pressing in a fraction, only to pull away again, giving him another swipe.

Lawson pushed up so he knelt on the bed and turned his head. An angry, frustrated flush covered his cheeks. "I need you to fuck me. So quit playing with my arse and bury your cock in it."

And there it was.

That filthy fucking mouth.

I put one hand on his shoulder and pushed him back down on the bed, leaving his arse raised. With my other hand, I lined my cockhead to his hole and pushed in.

There was no filthy mouth now, just short gasping breaths that became a long keening sound the deeper I pushed in. "That what you wanted?"

He cried out underneath me. "Yes, yes. Fuck yes."

I pulled out a little, only to push back in deeper, beginning to slowly thrust into him. He gasped and grunted with each breath, the most wonderful sounds. When I was buried to my balls inside him, I stayed there. I ran my hands over his shoulders, down his back, massaging him as I gave him time to adjust. He responded by rocking his hips, wordlessly asking for more.

"Oh God," he murmured. "You're so big."

"And you can take every inch," I said, thrusting into him sharply.

He let out a long low groan, but raised his arse. "I can feel your pulse inside me."

*Oh fucking hell.* His dirty mouth would be the end of me.

"Jack," he moaned. "Fuck me."

I thrust into him again and again, listening to his whimpers and moans, his whispered pleas for more. I was so close to coming. He felt so damn good, his arse was so warm and slick, but I needed to feel his mouth as well.

"I want to see you." I slowly pulled out. "Roll over."

He quickly did as I told him to and lifted his knees to his chest. I pushed into his welcoming heat in one thrust, watching his eyes flutter closed. His mouth gaped open at the intrusion.

I crushed my mouth to his, tangling my tongue against his. Lawson's hands went to my hair and then my jaw, and he held my face right where he wanted me.

He kissed me deeply until he needed air. "God, you're so far inside me."

Lawson's words made my balls ache. I slammed into him, and his neck corded with strain. I grunted as I spoke. "If you keep talking like that, you'll make me come."

"Fuck yes." Lawson's arms tightened around me. "So good, Jack. This is what I need."

"You need to come first," I said, pushing up to lean on my left hand. I took his cock into my right hand and pumped him. Precome pulsed from his tip, so I ran my thumb through it, slicking his shaft.

"Oh fuck," Lawson cried out. His hands fisted the sheets at his side. I drilled into him, fucking his arse as I pumped his cock. Then his eyes went wide and his mouth fell open. His whole body went taut, and his cock throbbed in my hand before shooting stripes of come across his belly as lightning struck somewhere close.

I pushed every inch into him, spreading his legs wider and fucking his mouth with my tongue while he rode out his orgasm on my cock.

But the need, the urgency was gone, and I could take my time now. When he sagged, sated and smiling, I let go of his cock and leaned over him. I thrust slower, deeper now his body was pliable and relaxed. He put his hand to my face and we kissed as I made love to him. Rocking slowly, savouring every second of being inside him. My climax built, slow and steady, and Lawson held my face as I came.

He gasped as I filled the condom deep within him. "I can feel every pulse," he whispered, his eyes wide with wonder. Then he kissed me as my orgasm rocketed through me.

I collapsed on top of him and he held me tight as my breathing returned to normal. What I experienced wasn't just a physical release. Something inside me shifted as well. I was pretty sure my heart had fallen for him.

I could feel his heartbeat against my chest, and I wondered if—I hoped—he felt the same.

Lawson's fingers traced patterns across my back, and I slowly pulled out of him. I rolled out of bed to discard of the condom, and he pulled up the blanket. When I came back, he smiled at my naked form and held the blanket open for me. I climbed in and he settled himself into the crook of my arm. I kissed the side of his head. "Want a shower?"

"No. Just want to lie here. Fall asleep with you."

I pulled away, and with my fingers under his chin, I tilted his face so I could look into his eyes. "Are you staying the night?"

He smiled at me. "Is that a problem?"

I tucked him back into my arms and snuggled in. "No problem at all."

He was quiet a minute, but I could tell by his breathing he was awake. "So um, sex with you is amazing."

129

I barked out a laugh. "I could say the same to you."

"Yes, you could."

I was still grinning. "Sex with you is amazing."

He sighed happily. "Thanks."

I kissed his forehead again as the rain fell outside. "It was better than amazing. You're better than amazing."

He froze before he lifted his head to look at me. "So are you."

His face was ethereal in the silver of the darkened room. I swallowed hard. "Tell me I'm not alone in what I feel."

He studied my face, searching for what, I don't know. "What do you feel?"

"That this is something special. That whatever this is shouldn't end when you go back to Melbourne."

His eyes bore into mine. "I don't want this to end."

"Me either."

"Promise me we'll work something out."

Thunder boomed outside, lightning split the sky as the storm raged. Outside, a frenzy whipped around us. Yet I'd never felt more calm, more peace than I did in that moment. "I promise." I fluttered my eyelashes on his cheek, making him smile.

"You're the first person to ever give me butterfly kisses."

"Really? But you're a butterfly expert."

He kissed me softly, lingering, but pulled away with a sigh as he settled his head on my chest. "I came to Tasmania in search of an elusive species. And I found it. But never in my wildest dreams did I expect to find you. And I believe I found a type of butterfly that exists only in my belly which only makes itself known when I think of you. Though sometimes they lodge in my throat when I see you and they make breathing somewhat difficult."

I smiled at his way with words, tightened my hold on him and grinned at the ceiling. "Me too."

With Lawson in my arms and the storm raging outside, my body sated and feeling more content than I could ever remember, I fell asleep with a happy heart and what could possibly be a permanent smile.

* * *

I woke to a panic. My phone was ringing, my pager was beeping, and Rosemary was barking. I sat up, grabbed my phone to see it wasn't even five a.m. Lawson was now awake, sitting up beside me, looking confused and disoriented. I answered my phone.

It was my rural fire inspector, Tony Wells. His voice was loud and brusque.

"Jack! We've got a Category Three bushfire. She's in Oxberry. 10k northeast of Scottsdale, but mate, she's heading straight for you."

# CHAPTER TWELVE

## *Lawson*

Jack shot out of bed. "Lawson, you need to get up. Get dressed. We need to leave."

"Why? What's happening?" I asked, getting out of bed. I rummaged through my bag and found some briefs and my jeans. I pulled on a shirt and found some socks.

Jack quickly dressed in long pants and a T-shirt. He pulled on his work boots. "There's a bushfire. I have to go."

"Where to?"

"RFS headquarters. In town."

He was starting to scare me. "Where's the fire?"

"Ten kilometres northeast of town. Oxberry Forest Reserve. Must have been a lightning strike."

I stopped and stared at him. "Jack, the butterflies…"

He let his hands fall to his sides and gave me a sad smile. "Hopefully we'll have it under control by the time it gets that close."

I shook my head. "But Jack—"

"I need you to go into town. Scottsdale has a fire exclusion zone surrounded by kilometres of cultivated farmland. You'll be safe there. Head straight for the community hall. It's the town's evacuation centre. That's where everyone will be. I need you to go there. Take Rosemary. I don't want her to freak out here by herself."

All I could do was stare.

Jack came over to me and put his hands on my shoulders. "Can you do that?"

I nodded. "I'm scared."

He gave me a quick hug and kissed the side of my head. "I know. But we'll have it all sorted soon. You'll be fine. Just stay in town with the others. The evac centre gets all the newest updates, so you'll know everything as it happens. But if you want to leave for Launceston, go now."

I shook my head. "No. I'll go to the evacuation centre." I knew his house was on the opposite side of town to the forest reserves, but I had to ask. "What about your house?"

"The house'll be fine. Well, if the fires reach here, it means all of Scottsdale is gone, and if that happens, my house will be the least of my worries."

"What about you?"

"I'll be fine. I've done this a hundred times before."

"Jack…"

He lifted my chin and kissed my lips. "I need to go."

He gave me a butterfly kiss that stole my breath. His lip quirked in a smile before he went for the door, but I stopped him. "Jack. Be safe."

He smiled at me. "Always." Then he stopped and gave Rosemary a pat. "You stay with Lawson, okay sweetheart?" He gave me a final look. "Go find Remmy. She'll be at the evac centre feeding people. It's what she does."

And with that, he was gone.

I stood there until I couldn't hear his ute in the distance anymore, frozen to the spot. Rosemary whined at me and it kicked me into gear. I pulled on my boots, grabbed my jacket and my phone, waited for Rosemary to join me, and pulled the front door shut behind me.

"Come on, girl," I said, calling for her to get into the Defender. I didn't bother with the harness. I let her sit in the front passenger seat. I needed to keep her close. I threw the Defender into first gear and roared my way into town.

Scottsdale was well and truly up and awake, even though it was barely five thirty in the morning. Cars, trucks, and people were all out, and already there was a line of cars at the community centre. I slowed down, someone was directing traffic, but I didn't stop.

I couldn't.

I turned off the main street onto North Scottsdale Road and drove like a bat out of hell in the direction of the bushfire.

* * *

I drove by cars who flashed their lights at me, but I didn't care. I couldn't just sit there and do nothing. I'd finally found a species of butterfly never seen before, and I couldn't allow it to be wiped off the face of the planet. Not without trying.

I barely slowed down to take the dirt road turn off, and I put my left hand out to brace Rosemary as she tried to keep her balance on the seat. "Almost there," I told her.

As day broke, the clouds were still dark and heavy but the rain had stopped. I could see now why Jack was concerned about the roads after the deluge we got yesterday because they were in pretty bad shape.

The ride was bumpy and we jostled around a bit and slid in the mud, but I could handle it, and the Defender was made for this. I sped past the areas I'd searched the day before, took one corner too fast and slid across the slick muddy road. Instead of hitting the brakes, I accelerated and overcorrected through the turn and we fishtailed out of what could have been a hairy situation.

"It's okay, we're good," I told Rosemary. Or myself. I wasn't sure at this point. My heart was in my throat.

I went past the spot we'd had lunch yesterday and took the Defender onto the road where Jack had taken me. The trees were rain-heavy and scraped up the sides of the Defender, and when I came to the gate, I didn't stop.

I simply ploughed right through it.

"Sorry," I told no one. I'd be up for a new gate. *If Jack forgives me. If I make it out of here alive.*

*Bloody hell, Lawson. You get yourself into some crazy predicaments.*

I pulled the Defender up to a stop at the end of the trail, and leaving my door open, I raced to the back and opened the rear door. All my plastic tubs filled with files and papers and equipment were there, somewhat tossed about. I picked up the closest one, pulled the lid off, and upended the contents onto the floor of the Defender.

I grabbed the now-empty container, Jack's shovel, which he'd left with me, and ran for the *Bursaria* bush. Rosemary ran along with me, and I wasted no time. I dug the shovel into the ants' nest, putting my foot on the shoulder of the blade and dug it into the nest as far as I could. I levered out a chunk of the nest and dumped it, mostly intact, into the tub.

Ants scurried en masse, but I picked up the tub and ran back to the Defender. I slid it into the back and quickly got the lid closed and locked it. I took another tub, upended the barometric equipment into the back of the Defender. Then I did a second tub, which had pruning gear in it, snatched up a pair of secateurs, and ran back to the *Bursaria* bush.

I searched the underside of the shrub and carefully snipped some branches off where butterflies were seeking protection from the weather underneath. I gently placed them in one tub and secured the lid.

I looked up at the sky then, and in that one moment I took to think, I heard it.

It was distant, far off but frightening all the same.

It was a quiet roar, like a background noise. Rumbling and angry. It wasn't thunder.

It was fire.

I had no clue how close it was. But there was something missing too. There were no birds. Yesterday they'd been so loud, but now there was nothing. I looked up at the sky again. I couldn't see smoke yet, but I guessed if I could see smoke this close, it would be too late.

Realising I was out of time, I picked up the shovel and edged it into the soil around the circumference of the shrub. I needed to try and be gentle, but the urgency didn't permit it. With as much force as I could muster, I pushed the shovel in, as careful of the roots as I could be, trying to get underneath the bulk of root growth. When I'd levered it the best I could, I reached into the stalk of the shrub and pulled.

I ended up on my arse, but the shrub had dislodged and a kaleidoscope of butterflies took to the wing. Some resettled, some fluttered away. "I'm sorry. I'm sorry," I told them. "I'm trying to save you."

Picking up the empty tub, I plonked the roots of the shrub into it and carried it back to the Defender. I slid it onto the floor of the backseat, trying to do as little damage as possible. I raced back to where the first tub and shovel were still lying on the ground, and Rosemary leapt along beside me.

"Your father's going to kill me," I told her.

I collected the tub with the butterflies in it, then everything else I could carry and hauled them back to the Defender. I loaded it all in and shut the back door. I closed the rear passenger door, cringing as some of the *Bursaria* got caught in the door.

I turned to call for Rosemary, but she wasn't at my feet. I scanned the clearing and found her at the edge of the gully.

"Rosemary, come!" I yelled. She didn't move. I patted my thighs and whistled. "Rosemary!" She looked at me, so I knew she'd heard, but she wasn't coming. "Goddammit, we don't have time for this."

Ignoring the huge plume of black smoke billowing into the sky, I ran over to her, fully intending to grab her by her collar or the scruff of her neck if I had to. But as I got closer, she disappeared down into the gully.

"Rosemary!" I yelled, anger and impatience in my tone.

As I got to the embankment, I saw where she'd gone. She was standing near the Tasmanian devil den. "Rosemary, come on."

She barked at me.

"Are you Lassie?"

She wagged her tail.

No one was ever going to believe me.

I ran down the embankment, and as I got closer to her, she started to dig at the den. Then she barked in it.

Something hissed back at her, which couldn't ever be a good thing, and she backed up. One of the little devil joeys came out, gnashing its teeth in a half ounce of might and fury.

"Oh, Jesus."

I couldn't leave it here to burn to death. I didn't know much about Tasmanian devil dens but I knew enough about bushfires, and everything to the depth of a metre of the surface was about to get baked.

Including us, if we didn't get going.

"Fuck, fuck, fuck."

I scrambled back up the edge of the gully, making a mental note to tell Jack that I'd just cursed and it had nothing to do with sex. Which was such an idiotic thought considering I might be rendered to cinder at any moment.

I raced back to the Defender and grabbed the last storage tub. I pulled the lid off and upended the papers inside it, grabbed the lid, and raced back to the gully.

"I have no idea what I'm doing," I mumbled as I flew over the edge and almost fell down the embankment. "Bloody hell. What would Jack do?"

*He'd take off his coat and throw it over the joey.*

Right. I shook out of my jacket and patted Rosemary to calm her and possibly myself. The joey was still out of the den, and I held the jacket out, slowly stepping in toward it. It backed up a little, growling and screeching. I threw the jacket, but the joey scampered back into the den.

Great. Well, it wasn't going to come back out in a hurry.

Rosemary barked at it, and how she sensed the urgency I'll never know. But she understood. And so did I. "One more attempt, then we have to go, okay?"

Okay, then. "What would Jack do now?" I looked at Rosemary and she looked back at me. I nodded. "Jack would get his arse out of here, that's what Jack would do."

*Think, Lawson.* What would a Tasmanian devil do?

It would bite the shit out of whatever tried to grab it.

With that as my only game plan, I rolled the jacket around my right fist as best I could, then got down on my knees at the entrance of the den and did the stupidest thing I'd ever done. I stuck my hand in.

Somewhere in my brain remembered an odd fact I'd heard as a child. *A Tasmanian devil has the jaw strength to pulverise its prey. Even joeys.*

I shook my head and mumbled to myself, "If I survive this, I should have my IQ retested."

The snarling and growling sounds erupted—there had to be more than one—and a second later, a dull, vice-like pressure latched on my fist, so I slowly, slowly pulled it out. Attached by its teeth to the end of my jacket was a joey, no bigger than a kitten, but its grip was like that of a pit bull terrier.

I spun on my knees to the tub and put the joey in it. Not knowing how to get it to let go, I gently pinched the scruff of its neck the way the mother would, and he let go. I quickly put the lid on and rewrapped my hand. I stuck it into the den a second time. There was more growling, then again something latched onto my jacket. I pulled out the second joey and put it in the tub with the first one.

The den was quiet. There was no more noise, no scurrying, no anything. Not from the den anyway. The sound of the fire was louder, closer. I opened the jacket up, and taking the lid off the tub, I covered the joeys and closed the lid again.

I looked up at the sky and saw smoke. Thick black smoke had crept over the trees. "Oh God."

I scrambled to my feet just as something else got Rosemary's attention. Her ears pricked up and she took off up the embankment just as I heard something else.

"Lawson!"

I clambered up the edge of the gully, trying to keep the tub even, but my foot kept slipping in the mud.

"Lawson!"

It was Jack.

Rosemary had disappeared over the top and I knew he'd see her, but I called out anyway. "Down here!"

Jack appeared in bright orange overalls looking a horrid mess. "Oh, thank god," he said with tears in his eyes. He put his hand to his heart before he held it out to me to help me up.

"Take the tub," I urged, holding it up. "Be careful with it."

He got down on his knees and took it, then helped pull me to the top. But he didn't stop. He picked up the tub, handed it to me, grabbed me by the shirt, and pulled me in the direction of the Defender. "Run!"

So I ran.

Rosemary went with Jack, and I struggled to start the Defender, my hands were shaking so badly. Jack reversed like a mad man and I finally got the gearstick into reverse and floored it. He spun his ute around onto the road, backed up a bit, and waited for me to do the same. When I reversed onto the road, I spun the Defender around, rammed it into first gear, and drove the fastest I'd ever driven. Jack's front bumper was right on my tail, he was urging me to go faster. Or at the very least, not letting me slow down.

Then I saw why.

In my rear-vision mirror, the tree line behind us was a wall of black smoke and orange fire.

* * *

The drive back into Scottsdale didn't take long. Given the speed at which we were travelling, it wasn't too surprising. It was long enough for the adrenaline to nose dive, and by the time I pulled up at the evacuation centre, I was barely holding it together.

There were people everywhere, and Jack's ute screeched to a stop behind me. I fumbled with my seatbelt, then couldn't get the door open at first, and when I did, I almost fell out of the Defender.

Jack stomped toward me. "What the hell were you thinking?!"

Right, then. His adrenaline had worn off too, but instead of falling in a heap like me, he was angry. No, actually, he was *pissed*. At me. And rightly so. Everyone had stopped and stared at our dramatic entrance.

He seemed so big and so intimidating, and his ire was aimed right at me. "For a genius, you can be really fucking stupid."

I nodded and my vision blurred as tears spilled down my cheeks. "I had to save them."

His whole body sagged, and he took huge strides so he could throw his arms around me. In front of all the good people of Scottsdale, he hugged me so damn hard, and all I could do was cry. My hands were shaking and, no, not just my hands. My whole body was shaking.

"I need a blanket here," he called out. He rubbed my back. He whispered against my ear. "You're okay, Lawson. I'm sorry I spoke to you like that. I was so worried, and you scared the hell outta me."

A blanket was placed around my shoulders, and I turned to find a concerned Remmy. She rubbed my arm. "You okay, hun?"

I nodded. I felt rather foolish for letting my emotions get the better of me. I wiped my face. "Sorry. I think the adrenaline wore off." I stepped back so I could look up into

Jack's face. "There were only two joeys. The mother and the other joey weren't there."

"Maybe the mother took the strongest," Jack suggested. Then he blinked. "Is that what you have in the tub?"

I nodded. "We need to take them to someone who can care for them. And the butterflies and eggs. I need to get them into a controlled environment."

Jack fixed the blanket around me, then collected the tub off the front passenger seat. He carefully pulled the lid off to reveal two little devil joeys huddled in my jacket. The people gathered around all oooohed and ahhhhed, but I couldn't take my eyes off Jack. "Oh, Lawson," he whispered. "You went back for them?"

"Rosemary made me. She's really Lassie, did you know that?" She was sitting faithfully at our feet, so I took a second to give her a pat. "It was her idea to save the joeys. She was barking at them and wouldn't come back when I called her, and I would have died before I left her behind."

Jack's eyes shone with tears. I got the feeling he didn't get too choked up all that often. All he did was nod, then gave me a hard kiss on the side of my head. He looked at Remmy. "Can you stay with him? Make sure he doesn't run off and almost die trying to save any more animals. I'll go and see if I can find Paul."

Remmy nodded and gave me a bit of a hug. We watched Jack leave with the tub of devil joeys. "Who's Paul?"

"Paul's a local wildlife rescue guy. He looks after native animals until they're ready for release."

"Oh. Okay."

Remmy gave me a sad smile. "Oh, Lawson, you should have seen Jack. They got the fire contained on the southeast line, so he came here looking for you. I told him I hadn't seen you at all, and he took off like… crazy. He just turned and ran. I guess he knew where to look for you."

Jack was suddenly back with a man who was now holding the tub with the two joeys. Jack gave me a look that said I was in a lot of trouble. "Oh, I knew where to look alright. And when I saw the gate on the reserve had been smashed off its hinges, I knew exactly where to find him."

"I'll pay for the gate," I said.

"Never mind the gate now," Jack said. "That whole area's now nothing but charred ground. There's no gate or fences anymore."

"The fire," I said, looking to the east. The hills were nothing but dark clouds and black smoke. "How was it contained? It didn't look too contained when we were in the mountains. And why are we not evacuating?"

"We pushed the frontline to run up the mountain, making it turn back on itself," Jack explained. "The two kilometres of cleared farming land between the town and the national park protects the town."

Paul, the man holding the joey tub spoke then. "You got these two little critters out?" People had gathered around, all clearly curious.

I nodded. "I think the mother and other joey left or died. I don't know, but these two were all that was there. I'm sorry if I wasn't supposed to interfere, but Rosemary wouldn't let me leave them."

Paul looked down at the dog and smiled. "Always liked your dog, Jack." Then Paul looked at me again. He offered me his free hand, which I shook. "You did real good, thank you. We'll get these two checked over by the vet and cared for until they can be released."

I was getting teary again. "Thank you."

Jack put his arm around me and pulled me against him. "Did you save the butterflies?"

"I hope so." I looked up at him. "I need to leave for Launceston. Now."

Remmy was somehow now holding a cup of tea and a sandwich. She handed them both to me. "Eat."

I took them gratefully. I hadn't realised how hungry I was... Jack went to the Defender and opened the back door. Remmy, Rosemary, and I followed him. There were papers and equipment and books and stuff everywhere. But the two tubs were the most important.

"I collected ants and some live butterflies," I said, speaking around my mouthful of food.

Then Jack opened the rear passenger door to reveal the entire *Bursaria* shrub. "And this?"

"I had to improvise."

Remmy laughed, then looked closer to the floor of the Defender. "Are they ants? Oh God, there's ants everywhere."

"They don't bite," Jack and I said in unison, making us all smile.

"What kind of butterflies are they?" Paul asked.

"Well, they don't have a name...," I said, finishing my tea. "They're a new species."

He stared at me. "Wow. Now I can see why you risked your life to save them."

I nodded, and Jack sighed. I realised this whole me-almost-dying and him-almost-dying-to-save-me might be somewhat of a bone of contention. I frowned. "I am sorry."

He put his hand around my neck and pulled me close. He didn't seem to care it was in front of everyone, so neither did I. I looked up at him. "I need to get the butterflies and eggs to Professor Tillman. He'll have the equipment to save them."

Jack nodded. "I'll drive."

Just then, the clouds opened and rain poured from the sky and people cheered and hugged one another around us. Paul took the joeys, Remmy took Rosemary and ran for cover, and I climbed into the front passenger seat. Jack was already behind the wheel and he leaned over, grabbed my face, and kissed me hard. The windows were all obscured by rain and I doubted anyone saw. I didn't care if they did. "Thank God you're okay," he whispered before putting the Defender into first and driving out of Scottsdale.

* * *

The drive to Launceston started off quiet. The seriousness of what I'd done, how I'd put both our lives in danger, was starting to weigh on me. "I really am sorry," I said quietly. "But I had to try."

Jack's hands squeezed the steering wheel. "I hate to think what would have happened if I hadn't found you…"

I nodded slowly. "I know."

"Do you?" he asked seriously.

"Yes. I would have died and Rosemary too because I'd put her in danger as well. She had no choice where I took her, and I'm sorry."

Jack looked at me for a long moment and shook his head. "I'm talking about you. *You*, Lawson. I'm not sure what I'd do if…" He swallowed hard and left the rest of his sentence unsaid.

I held out my hand for his, and when he grabbed hold, I threaded our fingers and squeezed his palm. "Thank you for saving my life today." I lifted his hand and kissed his knuckles. His hands were blackened and dirty, but I didn't care. I kissed them again. "Thank you."

"Just promise me you won't do it again."

I thought about that and licked my lips. "I can't promise because I can't say with certainty that I won't be put in a similar circumstance. If I were to have to choose—"

"Lawson," he interrupted sternly. "The correct answer is I promise."

"I was going to say, if I were ever in a position again where I had to choose between my life and that of a defenceless animal, well, that's really not a choice."

"Thank you."

I looked out the window because I was very certain we were thinking different outcomes.

He sighed, long and loud. "You'd choose the animal, wouldn't you?"

144

I quickly turned to look at him. "Well, there are many varying factors in this scenario, and I can't hypothesise to one conclusion…"

He started to smile, and I stopped talking. "What?" he asked.

"Why are you smiling at me?"

"Because you're adorable. Incredibly frustrating, possibly infuriating, but completely adorable."

I huffed and sank back in the seat. Still holding his hand, I lifted it to press the back of his hand to my cheek. "And you're kind of wonderful."

* * *

We pulled up at the address Professor Tillman had given me when I'd called to let him know what had happened.

He met us out the front of his house, where I made introductions. It was an older style weatherboard home with perfectly maintained gardens, and a single glass butterfly graced the wall by the front door. "Welcome," he said. "Looks like you've both had quite an adventure this morning. Saw it all on the news."

"Yes, quite." And we were a mess. I was covered in dirt and mud from the gully embankment, and Jack was still wearing his soot-covered RFS overalls. I opened the back door to the Defender and handed the professor the lighter tub. I handed Jack the heavier one, filled with a shovel full of *Notoncus* ant nest. I grabbed the shrub from the back seat.

"Come this way," Professor Tillman said.

We followed him around the side of his home to what looked like a garden hot house, but I smiled when I saw it. "Oh, this is magnificent."

The professor basically had his own butterfly house in his backyard.

"It's not bad," he said modestly, walking inside first.

145

I dumped the tub with the *Bursaria* shrub in it by the inside of the door, with Jack one step behind me. The professor slid the tub onto a workbench, and slowly took the lid off. He gently lifted out one of the offcuts of shrub and turned it over. There was one butterfly on it, and it spread its wings in greeting.

The professor laughed. "Well, hello to you too."

As it turned out, only four survived. The bottom of the tub was a graveyard for five fully grown butterflies. My heart sank. "I tried to save them all," I mumbled.

Jack rubbed my back. His gentle, wordless reassurance meant so much.

"There are eggs in the roots of the shrub," I said. "Hopefully they survived."

The professor beamed. "You did a remarkable thing today." He went over to the shrub and squatted down beside it. He inspected the mass of roots and dirt and ants for a long minute before he looked up and smiled. "I think you saved the entire order of species, son."

After we'd secured the four remaining butterflies into a holding tank and the eggs had been safely relocated into hatching nets, it was afternoon. I could barely keep my eyes open. After a day of such adrenaline, I was starting to crash.

"We've done all we can do today," the professor said. "You should get some rest. Tomorrow we can decide where we go from here."

I nodded, knowing he was right. "Oh, and Professor Asterly has told me he expects to be let in on the discovery. I told him to politely sod off."

Jack snorted. "I heard that conversation. It wasn't exactly polite."

I shrugged and Professor Tillman laughed. "That's the reason I asked you to find this butterfly, son. That tenacity right there. Not that any other lepidopterist would probably have stared down a raging bushfire to save a butterfly either, mind you. But I knew I liked you from the moment I read your dissertation, which could have been subtitled

146

'Everything The Butterfly Association's Doing Wrong Because They're a Bunch of Idiots.'"

"You didn't?" Jack scoffed and looked at me with wide eyes. I shrugged.

"Yes, he most certainly did," the professor answered. "Best thing I ever read. I told the commissioner for endangered species something similar back in '78, so I knew you and I would get along just fine."

I found myself smiling at the old man. "Sometimes people need to hear things they'd rather not hear. It doesn't mean they shouldn't be said."

He grinned. "Exactly."

I fought another yawn, and Jack shook Professor Tillman's hand. "It was a pleasure to meet you, but I better get him home or he'll be asleep on the floor."

"Yes, this day is catching up with me," I admitted. "But I'll be back after breakfast. Thank you, Professor Tillman."

He smiled. "Thank *you*. The butterfly'd be lost if it weren't for you. And please, call me Warner." Then he paused. "And you better get thinking on a name to call it. The butterfly, that is. You found it, you name it."

*What?* "Oh, no… I couldn't do that. And anyway, I'd have never found it if it weren't for you. Actually, I wouldn't have found it if it weren't for Jack. He took me to look at some Tasmanian devil joeys and that's when I found them. But I wouldn't have even been in Tasmania if it weren't for you."

Warner put his hand up like it was final. "You found it, you name it."

"Then I shall name it the Tillman Copper, after the man who found it first."

Professor Tillman's eyes got watery and he cleared his throat. "Well, then I'll be honoured."

I beamed at him.

As we were leaving, he waved his hand at the shrub I'd dug out of the mountainside and bought with us. "You boys take the *Bursaria*. I've got plenty of it here. Plant this one somewhere, see what it might attract."

I smiled at Jack. "I know the perfect place."

# CHAPTER THIRTEEN

## *Jack Brighton*
## *Two weeks later*

Life in the last two weeks had been interesting and life-changing, that was for sure. Lawson hadn't gone back to Melbourne. Given the Tillman Copper was granted new species status, much to his boss Asterly's disgust, Lawson was the lead lepidopterist in charge of the find.

When his boss had tried to derail Lawson's role, Lawson had simply contacted the head of the University department, and the chairman of the Butterfly Association and told them both exactly how it was going to go.

He *would be* staying in Tasmania to establish a research and protection study on the Tillman Copper. He *would be* lead lepidopterist, and he *would* have their full cooperation. No questions, no arguments.

So that was that.

I couldn't have been happier. Because it meant he was staying in Tasmania.

I asked him to move in with me. I'd told him I was falling in love with him, and he'd kissed and hugged me in return, telling me he felt the same. *The butterflies he felt when he saw me had morphed into love*, he'd said. *The most remarkable metamorphosis*. His words made my heart sing.

But he'd decided that it was too soon for us to move in together. I understood his reasoning—we'd only known each other for three weeks, after all—but I was a little disappointed.

When I'd seen him that time sitting on my lounge room floor in his PJs with Rosemary asleep at his side, I wanted it on a permanent basis. And when I'd thought he might die in the bushfires, my priorities, and my heart, had never been clearer. But he'd said not yet, and I respected his decision.

He'd found a place to rent in Launceston and was having his things ferried over. And in the meantime, he would stay with me until it all arrived, which it did a week later. The week he was at my house was incredible, even he agreed. We talked, we laughed, we cooked, and the sex was amazing. But he didn't want to rush things and ruin what could be something incredible. He did plant that *Bursaria* shrub near the rosemary by the northern side of my house, though, which in a Lawson-Gale way was almost a promise that he'd be around long-term. If butterflies would take a year or two to roost there or even ten years, it gave me hope that he'd be there to see it.

But Launceston was where his work was, so it made sense for him to live there. I told myself it was a helluva lot closer than Melbourne, and the forty-five-minute drive wasn't too bad. We'd only spent a few nights apart in the second week, and while it allowed me to concentrate on my work, I did miss him.

But he'd invited me, and Rosemary of course, to stay for the weekend, and when I arrived on Friday night, he welcomed me with one hell of an amazing kiss. "How was work?"

"Busy. We've got damage control and regeneration plans to implement," I said, kissing him again. The week after the bushfire, I'd taken him back to the place he'd found the Tillman Copper. The whole area was a razed, blackened landscape. Nothing was left, and it was a sobering reminder of how close he'd come to being killed. "Will be flat out for the next twelve months. How about you?"

He gave me an eye-crinkling smile. "Great. There's something I want to show you tomorrow."

"Don't want to show me tonight?"

He shook his head, and taking my hand, he led me to his bedroom. "Nope. There's something else I want to do tonight."

"Oh yeah? What's that?"

"You."

* * *

After he'd cooked me breakfast, we got dressed and he took me back to Warner Tillman's house. I'd been here a few times, but Lawson had been here every day. He walked around the side of the house with a familiar ease when Warner called out to us. "In here, boys."

Lawson went straight inside, with a skip in his step. He was so excited, and seeing him lead his own team and push for the ecological betterment of a species was a spectacular thing to witness. "Anything yet?"

"Any minute now."

I looked between them. "Any minute *what* now?"

Lawson pulled me over to a glass case where inside was a net with a cocoon attached to it. "What you're looking at is the chrysalis of the Tillman Copper. We're about to witness what no other person in the world has seen. The very first Tillman Copper to emerge, imago."

"Emargo-what?"

"Imago. It's the final and fully developed adult stage. When a caterpillar emerges as a butterfly."

I smiled at him. It was kind of like him. I was finally getting to see him in his element, doing what he was born to do. He'd spent years as a caterpillar, with his head down, working hard and going unnoticed. But now... now he had wings, and the world could see he was truly a magnificent man. I kept that analogy to myself, though. For now.

Then, as if right on cue, the chrysalis moved and started to split. A small copper coloured butterfly entered the world, imago.

It was incredible.

I looked at Lawson then, at his face, at the look of wonder and amazement in his eyes, and what he saw in the butterfly, I saw in him.

Lawson Gale, imago.

~ *the end*

# SPECIAL MENTION

I'd like to offer a heartfelt thanks to Julie Bozza. For offering her support, feedback, and input for Imago.

Readers, if you enjoyed Imago, please do yourself a favour and pick up Julie's Butterfly Hunter. You won't be disappointed.

Nicholas and Dave are gorgeous.

# About the Author

N.R. Walker is an Australian author, who loves her genre of gay romance.
She loves writing and spends far too much time doing it, but wouldn't have it any other way.

She is many things: a mother, a wife, a sister, a writer. She has pretty, pretty boys who live in her head, who don't let her sleep at night unless she gives them life with words.

She likes it when they do dirty, dirty things... but likes it even more when they fall in love.

She used to think having people in her head talking to her was weird, until one day she happened across other writers who told her it was normal.

She's been writing ever since...

# Contact N.R. Walker

Email:
nrwalker@nrwalker.net

# Also by N.R. Walker

*Blind Faith*
*Through These Eyes (Blind Faith #2)*
*Blindside: Mark's Story (Blind Faith #3)*
*Ten in the Bin*
*Point of No Return – Turning Point #1*
*Breaking Point – Turning Point #2*
*Starting Point – Turning Point #3*
*Element of Retrofit – Thomas Elkin Series #1*
*Clarity of Lines – Thomas Elkin Series #2*
*Sense of Place – Thomas Elkin Series #3*
*Taxes and TARDIS*
*Three's Company*
*Red Dirt Heart*
*Red Dirt Heart 2*
*Red Dirt Heart 3*
*Red Dirt Heart 4*
*Red Dirt Christmas*
*Cronin's Key*
*Cronin's Key II*
*Cronin's Key III*
*Exchange of Hearts*
*The Spencer Cohen Series, Book One*
*The Spencer Cohen Series, Book Two*
*The Spencer Cohen Series, Book Three*
*Blood & Milk*
*The Weight Of It All*
*Perfect Catch*
*Switched*

## Free Reads
*Sixty Five Hours*
*Learning to Feel*
*His Grandfather's Watch (And The Story of Billy and Hale)*
*The Twelfth of Never (Blind Faith 3.5)*
*Twelve Days of Christmas (Sixty Five Hours Christmas)*

## Translated Titles

*Fiducia Cieca (Italian translation of Blind Faith)*
*Attraverso Questi Occhi (Italian translation of Through These Eyes)*
*Preso alla Sprovvista (Italian translation of Blindside)*
*Il giorno del Mai (Italian translation of Blind Faith 3.5)*
*Cuore di Terra Rossa (Italian translation of Red Dirt Heart)*
*Cuore di Terra Rossa 2 (Italian translation of Red Dirt Heart 2)*

*Confiance Aveugle (French translation of Blind Faith)*
*A travers ces yeux: Confiance Aveugle 2 (French translation of Through These Eyes)*
*Aveugle: Confiance Aveugle 3 (French translation of Blindside)*
*À Jamais (French translation of Blind Faith 3.5)*
*Cronin's Key (French translation)*
*Cronin's Key II (French translation)*
*Au Coeur de Sutton Station (French translation of Red Dirt Heart)*
*Partir ou rester (French translation of Red Dirt Heart 2)*

*Rote Erde (German translation of Red Dirt Heart)*

S
ᒪᓦ

Made in the USA
Lexington, KY
29 March 2017